Inside the
Heart of
Hope

Inside the Heart of Hope

RISHABH PURI

Srishti
PUBLISHERS & DISTRIBUTORS

Srishti Publishers & Distributors
Registered Office: N-16, C.R. Park
New Delhi – 110 019
Corporate Office: 212A, Peacock Lane
Shahpur Jat, New Delhi – 110 049
editorial@srishtipublishers.com

First published by
Partridge in 2016

Revised version, 2017
First published by
Srishti Publishers & Distributors in 2017

Acknowledgements

Every day is a miracle. A chance for your fortunes to change, blessings to fall upon you like rain. Every day you might see a new mercy, sing a new song, or feel joy like you've never felt before. I am thankful that today, you've picked up my novel and have decided to read it.

Not every day of my life has been one blessed with health and good fortune. But out of it has come the ability to write truths, a deeper appreciation for the life I live, and above all, an overwhelming gratitude for the people with whom I share this life. I'm blessed with the opportunity to thank them, and I'd like to take that opportunity now.

First and foremost, I'd like to thank god for the overwhelming blessings he has graced me with, and the joy I've felt in this life. I would also like to thank my grandparents, my mother, father, and sister for their love and support throughout my whole life. Not everyone is as graced as I am with a family who loves and cares for me the way you do. Without you, I would be lost.

I would like to thank my doctors who have stood by my side and taken incredible risks to give me a full, healthy life, and find for me a reprieve from the pain I feel. Dr. Alok Suryavanshi – a friend, a brother and my guardian angel – thank you for the countless hours you've devoted to my case and your expertise. Also, thank you for making me laugh on some of the darkest days of my life. Your care for me has strengthened me beyond belief.

And finally, I would like to thank you, dear reader, for opening this book. It is not every day that gives birth to a project of passion. It is not every day that a man can wake up to see one of his dreams realized for all to see and enjoy. What you are reading today is a product of my passion, one of my dreams brought to life. So today is an incredible day. Thank you for reading. I hope you enjoy.

Foreword

My name is Rick... and I have a heart disorder. For much of my life, I reversed these two statements and felt that I was my disorder first and a person second. It has taken me many years to learn that I have my own identity, strengths, dreams, and hopes. I used to base my entire life on the fact that I had a disorder that affected my day-to-day life, and I tailored the way I lived accordingly.

I am not sure when that magical transition occurred where I changed from thinking that people could look at me and see that I was a manic depressive, but somehow, somewhere along the way, I began to look in the mirror and say, "I'm Rick... and I have many talents and things that I should be proud of."

I think that part of what makes a person go through life – thinking that the disorder is who they are – is the degree to which it can take over your life. This was particularly so for me as I had also become deeply embroiled in the mental health system – being in the hospital, seeing an endless parade of counsellors, and so on. It seems that everything I did and said was done with the consideration of how my actions could impact my illness. Having been disabled enough to receive disability benefits, I was also wrapped up in the struggle of how I was to make it financially every day. Add to this concern the physical and emotional side effects of the various medications, like weight gain, numb and fuzzy feelings. Life seemed like a bother and a pain, and self-image was a huge problem.

If pushed, I think the key to my recovery was my curiosity. Never having been content to be told that I had such and such a disability, I sought information. What was it I had, what was my prognosis, and what could I do about it?

So I embraced my curiosity and read. I devoured dozens, if not hundreds, of books, articles, and brochures. I wanted to know what was expected of me, or rather, what were the 'limitations' that everyone else assumed I'd have to live with because of my disability. This knowledge and the dissatisfaction with what people thought I would do created a fierce determination within myself that I was not going to live up to those expectations but was going to surpass, thrive, and grow beyond them. That was the beginning – the beginning of recovery and the road to personal growth and well-being.

I never took *no* for an answer. Some days were exceptionally tough, and even today, some days are horrible. There were days when I thought that throwing it all away and just letting things slip back into chronic hospitalizations and unhappy relationships would be far easier than fighting for a life. But I kept going. Once I found out all that I could about my disorder, I moved on. What were the resources available in the community, province, and nation that could come to my aid? I became vocal, and in whatever strange way, I became respected for not being afraid to speak out. I developed trust between others and myself so that even when I had a differing view on things, people knew that I was always open to considering other ideas.

This was a healing process too. It provided me with an avenue for sharing my experiences, my thoughts, and my feelings with others, with the end goal of healing, and all this with the hope of implementing change within the health system. I never expected to be the driving force behind big changes. As long as I could help one person, I would be happy.

Ever since, one thing has led to another. I started to take pride in who I was, how I looked, and what others thought of me. I also knew that even if others still couldn't accept me for who I was, then that was fine too.

The changes along the way have been dramatic. Twenty years ago, I was being hospitalized every six months, had no hope of having a fulfilling relationship with that significant someone, and my relationship with my family was non-existent. Now, I am happily married, working full-time, with strong family ties and involvement. Hospitalization is, for the most part, ancient history.

I have learned that when times are tough, I need to sit back and ask myself the following questions: Is it me? Is it my environment? Is it someone else's problem? Or is it my illness?

These questions, although not as dominant any more, run like a continuous loop in my subconscious. Learning to identify what it is that is going on and whether or not it is related to my illness has allowed me to make great strides in my life. Through the support of my family, a loving wife, an understanding doctor, a great work environment, friends who understand, and an all-round good support network, I have succeeded in carrying on with a 'normal' life. Medications have provided some assistance, but even with these, I have had to learn that they are not the answer to everything. I have had to learn to cope with things just as everyone else does, only that sometimes I must realize that I need a little extra help along the way.

Many times, people ask me if I would change who I am, and I always say 'No'. I wouldn't wish my disorder on anyone, but I wouldn't change it. I am happy with who I am. I have many regrets along the way to where I am now, but if I were to go back and change just one little thing, then who would I be now? No, I am happy with me, and if that's good enough for me, then I hope it's good enough for everyone else.

Prologue

There is a boy in the yard of the house I used to live in. He's smiling and running around, playing the way all nine-year-old boys play – all speed and motion. He's wearing a shirt just like the one I used to love at that age. He's climbing trees and laughing. The other kids on the playground are exactly the same, each equally dirty and perfectly happy with it.

His mother comes to call him in. She's smiling, happy that her son is out catching the rays of the sun.

The scene is familiar. In fact, I recognize every part of it. The woman who's smiling is my mother. And that little boy is me. I remember that day. Well, *remember* is too strong a word. It's like a really vivid dream that I had, one where you remember small details but it still doesn't seem quite real. The boy is me. But the idea of me being so carefree is... foreign. My mother's face without a hint of worry is surreal. And the breathless look of pure joy on my face is so far away that I have to remind myself that this is a *real* memory.

I remember running to my mother and her holding me in her arms and hugging me fiercely. I remember going into the parlour and meeting my father, who didn't think twice about a son covered in sweat and panting like a dog. I remember it all. You would think that I would long for days like that, but honestly, they're so far away that I can't. It's like longing for a fantasy you know is not real.

Besides, I know what happens at the end of that day.

Rick

"Good afternoon! Sorry for keeping you waiting."

The man in the white lab coat is my doctor. I've known him all my life, but he still freaks me out. My parents are always so sombre when they are with him. I still have no idea why. At least once a year, we come to this same office; he sticks that cold thing they use to check your heart to my chest (I think it's called a…a… ste…steto…stetoscoop?), asks me a bunch of dumb questions, and then we go home.

Last time was different though. The last time we were here, I had to do all these tests with these really cool machines. Some parts were kinda fun in a weird way. One of the machines was huge and circular, and the nurse told me they shoot rays at you so the doctors can see your insides. When I asked if anyone had ever become a superhero from being in the machine too long, she had laughed and said that she couldn't tell me. After all, superheroes' secret identities and powers had to stay secret. On another test, they attached all these things to me and had me run on this machine. It had made me very tired, so I guess I didn't have superpowers. It had been a cool day even though I didn't get powers from the circular machine.

Now my parents and I are sitting in the doctor's office, waiting for, as my mother calls them, 'test results'. I'm serious; the way she says it, you can actually hear the bold type and the quotes. The look on the doctor's face can't be good. He sits down and looks at me.

"How would you like to play some games, Rick?"

I shrug. I've been to their games room before. It was boring. Still, he picks up the phone and says into it, "Nurse, could you come take Rick to the games room?"

Soon the nurse who had taken me through all the tests comes in, takes my hand, and leads me to the games room down the hall. She leaves me with the nurse in charge of the games room with a smile.

The games room nurse isn't as nice as she is. And soon, she gets bored of watching kids play board games. As soon as she stops looking, I slip back to the doctor's office, opening it up a crack so I can hear what they are saying.

"I'm sorry to tell you this, but it seems like the hyperlipidaemia that we diagnosed when your son was young has caused him to develop aortic valve stenosis." He pauses and glances around the room before continuing. "Basically that means the opening of one of the valves that lead from his heart is narrower than usual."

There is silence in the room, and my mother bursts into tears. My father, on the other hand, always the protector, puts an arm around her and starts with the questions.

"What does that mean for him? How do we treat it?"

"The aorta is the artery that carries blood from the left ventricle of the heart to branch arteries. The narrowing was probably caused by the hyperlipidaemia that we had diagnosed when he was a child. Basically, the condition means that any physical activity puts a strain on his heart. We just have to monitor him and make sure that the condition doesn't worsen."

"What happens if it worsens?"

"There isn't a cure for this kind of disorder. If it gets worse, we may have to consider surgery…"

There is a swift intake of breath from my mother, and she asks, "He needs a new heart?"

The doctor shakes his head. "No, even if the condition worsens, we still only need to replace just the valve."

"How risky is the surgery, Doctor?" my father asks.

"Well, like all surgery, there is risk."

"Could he die?"

There is a pause. "Yes. I'm sorry. But keep in mind that it might never get to that point. We just need to play it safe. We will keep monitoring him. I recommend check-ups every six months. He could still live a full and happy life as long as he takes it easy and doesn't overexert himself."

The tap on my back startles me so much that I fall into the room. All three of them turn to look at me. When my mom realizes it's me, she runs to me and wraps me in her arms.

"Mom?"

"It's okay, honey, we're going to take care of you. Everything is going to be just fine." She turns to the doctor. "Can we take him home now?"

He nods, and she carries me out without another word.

"Mom! Mom!"

"*Rick*! How many times have I told you not to run?"

I slide to a stop. Ever since we've come back from the hospital, my mom's gone crazy. She makes the greatest fuss over every little thing. She never used to care if I ran in the house. Now she acts like it's a crime. I walk (as fast as I can).

"Mom, I'm going to be late for school!"

"You've never been this excited for school before. Does this mean you're going to bring home all 'A's this year?"

It is the first day of school after the summer break, and I am looking forward to it more than usual. It is a chance to get away from this new version of my mother. I love the woman, but lately, she has been driving me crazy.

"Mom, you know I always do my best in school."

She laughs. "I know, honey, just give me a minute. Let me grab my things."

I could barely hide the panic in my voice. "You're coming?"

She laughs. "Don't worry, I just have to talk to your teacher. Now come on. We don't have all day."

When we get to school, my mom leaves me to talk to my friends while she looks for my teacher. My best friend Jacob is already there and, as usual, is talking up a storm. He loves to tell everyone just what he did for the summer break. His dad is always taking him places, and he almost always brings back different candies from all the places.

"Rick!"

He leaves all the people surrounding him and runs to me.

"Hey, Jacob."

"Am I gonna beat you in the races again this year?"

I laugh. "Like a slow poke like you could beat me."

Every year at the first break of school, all the boys have a race. The winner gets bragging rights for the rest of the term. Jacob and I always compete against each other, whether or not we win. The last few terms he's been winning, and I am determined to regain my rightful title of being the faster of the two of us.

Just then, the bell rings, and we head to class.

As soon as we get there, the teacher calls my name and asks me to step outside with him.

"Rick, as you know, your mother came to see me."

I nod, wondering where he's heading with this.

"She told me that you have been to the doctor over the summer holiday?"

Again, I nod. I've learnt that not saying anything around teachers is the best way to stay out of trouble.

"Okay, because of what the doctor said, we are going to be making some changes to your break schedule. From now on, your break will last for thirty minutes instead of an hour. For the first thirty minutes, you'll sit in class with me. We can play board games or do anything you want. If anyone wants to sit with you, then you can invite them. Does that sound okay?"

I can barely answer him. Tears are forming in my eyes. Break is my favourite part of the day; having that taken away is just horrible. And taking away the first thirty minutes would just be torture. But I nod anyway; I've learnt it's impossible to argue with teachers.

We walk back into class with me in a daze. The next thing I know, the bell is ringing for break, and the class is emptying. One glance from my teacher lets me know that the whole thing isn't a joke. And for the next thirty minutes, I stare at the pages of my textbook and try not to cry.

"Sir, it's been thirty minutes. Can I go out now?"

He looks up and smiles. "Of course, Rick."

I run outside without pause, hoping I haven't missed too much of the race. I pull up to the finish line just in time to see Jacob finish first.

He's panting hard and with his hands on his knee. People are running up to him, screaming and whooping. I want to go to him, but I'm not really in the mood to celebrate. Still, he's my best friend, so I start to get closer. He looks up and sees me coming.

"Rick, I won!"

I grin at him. He's been trying to win this race for as long as I've known him, and I'm really happy for him.

"That's awesome! I knew you could do it! But you know what that means...?"

He stares at me in confusion.

"It means all I have to do is beat you to be the winner."

I grab his arm and pull him to the starting point. When we get there, I drop to one knee the way they do in the Olympics, except Jacob isn't next to me.

I look to see him looking away reluctantly.

"I can't race you, Rick."

"What? Why?"

"I don't want you to die."

"Die? What makes you think I'll die?"

"Teacher says that you're sick, and if you play too hard, you'll die."

And just like that, I knew this was going to be the most miserable school year of my life.

"But Mom, I don't understand. No one will play with me!"

The fight has been going on for about fifteen minutes. The whole time my mother has just been looking at me and shaking her head.

"It's for your own good, sweetheart. You're sick."

"But I feel fine."

"I know, honey, but you know those pains that you feel in your chest sometimes?"

I nod. I get them mostly after playing, but they aren't a big deal.

"Well, that's your body trying to tell you that it's sick."

"But I don't get them all the time."

"I know, but we have to be very careful."

"What if I promise not to get them anymore?" This time, I can't hide the tears.

My mom scoops me in her arms.

"Oh, honey…I know it's hard, but you just have to be patient. Your life is going to be different. I know it feels terrible right now, but it will be easier, I promise. Now, how about we get some ice cream to make you feel better?"

I frown, knowing that the discussion is over, but still let her take my hand and lead me to the kitchen.

Maybe if I had known how drastically my life was going to change, maybe I would have fought more. How was I to know that that was the first in a long line of miserable days.

The restaurant is drenched in sunlight. Rays of sunlight shoot through the windows and dart all around the inside of the restaurant. I'm sitting at a table, eating a plate of fries one at a time. Out of the corner of my eye, I notice an older woman sitting across a man that I assume is her husband. They're holding hands, talking, and laughing. For a moment, I wonder if I will ever reach that age. It has been years since my world was rocked by the news of my heart condition. I still go for check-ups every six months, and so far so good. I think of the woman I would want to be sitting with when I reach that age. Amy is everything I've ever wanted in a girl, beautiful and smart, and just the thought of her is enough to make me smile. We met in our freshman year of high school and have been together since then. We're even thinking of going to the same university when we graduate. My thoughts are interrupted by Amy, who, returning from the bathroom, flops into the booth and puts an arm around me.

"Whoa! Welcome back." I am a bit startled but quickly regain my composure. I don't want Amy to know what I am thinking about. I quickly grab a fry and throw it into my mouth.

"Did I scare you?" Amy smiles at me as she makes herself comfortable.

"Did you scare *me*?" I laugh out loud and shake my head in disagreement.

"Oh sure… sure. Liar!"

"Honest, I'm unscareable." Amy rolls her eyes, and her face then quickly changes to a more subdued expression. I know her well enough to know exactly what she is going to ask.

"So... have you thought about what we talked about last night? Coz I was really thinking about it. . . and. . . I think we should." I feel my throat tighten and my stomach instantly clench.

"Yah, me too."

"You don't have to. You know, I just think it'd be great for us to go to the same university, you know?" Amy looks nervous too.

I grab her hand and think about the couple sitting a few tables away from us. In that moment, I decide that I want that. The university is a great place, and it is perfect for the both of us. I hadn't said yes last night because as much as I love Amy, I haven't been able to tell her the full truth about me. In school it is easy to explain away the missed days and not participating in school activities. I know I should tell her, but the last thing I want is for her to start treating me like my parents do – like something damaged and broken, or worse, she could leave me. If we go to the same university, I won't be able to hide what's happening anymore. On the other hand, when I think of separating from her, a shudder passes through me. I squeeze her hand.

"I want to, Amy. I love you, and I want to spend the rest of my life with you." She looks over the table and smiles. I pull her close to me for a kiss, and just as our lips begin to meet, my phone rings and ruins the whole moment.

"Sorry..."

Amy laughs and settles back into her seat and grabs her drink. I notice Dr Michael's number on my screen.

"Uh-oh, could you give me a minute? I have to take this," I answer, and almost instantly, my mind is trying to figure out a quick way to end the conversation and finish what Amy and I are about to do.

"What's up, Doc?" Amy snickers and shakes her head. I love her smile and the way she laughs. I'm always trying to get her to smile or laugh or just relax whenever I can.

"Hi Rick. I really need you to come to the hospital, preferably within the next hour. I need to tell you something." Dr Michael sounds strange, as if he is hiding something or is nervous. I realize that this call may be more important than the usual calls I get from the doctor.

"Umm...sure Doc. I can be there in about a half an hour. Is everything all right?"

"I'll explain everything when you get here. I've already called your parents. They will meet us here. Please just come as soon as you can."

"Yes sir. I'm on my way." We both hang up at the same time, and I dart a glance at Amy.

She flashes me a puzzled look. "What was that about?" she asks, sensing that the call was about something serious.

"Umm...that was just my doctor. He says he needs to see me." I try to say it as nonchalantly as I can. Amy is starting to get worried, and I have to keep her calm.

She stops sipping her drink and looks straight at me. I can see the questions right behind her eyes. I don't want the moment ruined, so I laugh and stand up, pulling my wallet out and laying some money on to the table to cover the bill and the tip.

"I...you're okay, right?" she asks. I have no clue what Dr Michael is going to say, but I feel as good as I've ever felt. A little tired, but that was normal.

"Hey, listen, he's just probably going to tell me to 'take your vitamins' and mention something about how my next check up is *very* important. Don't worry. You won't be getting rid of me that easy. To prove it, you can come with me." I smile at her and watch her eyes soften. She smiles a small, timid smile, grabs my arm, and we walk outside towards my car.

The ride to the hospital is quiet. I'm trying to figure out how to tell her about my condition. Occasionally, Amy touches my knee or caresses my elbow. She can tell, even though I'm trying to hide it, that I'm nervous. I smile at her, trying to ease the worry that is obvious on her face. She kisses me on the cheek and rubs my shoulder. And I wonder, how will she deal with the news of my condition?

The hospital lobby is nearly empty. Amy sits next to me, holding my hand as we look around. Across from us are a young boy and his father. The father is filling out paperwork as the boy flips through a kid's magazine. A few seats over is a young woman with a bandage around her left arm. She's chewing her bottom lip and tapping her foot.

"Rick…?" The nurse calls from behind a half-opened door, her head stuck out along with her clipboard. Amy grabs my hand as if to make sure I won't leave her behind. I pull her towards me, and we walk into Dr Michael's office together.

Dr Michael is sitting in front of a computer and typing. When he hears the door open, he quickly swivels around in his office chair and greets us.

"Hello, Rick and…Amy, I presume."

"Hey, Doctor."

"Good Afternoon," we both answer.

Dr Michael looks from me to Amy and back again.

"Umm…not to be rude Amy, but I think it would be better if you could wait outside." I turn to face him as Amy stands up from the couch. I reach my hand out and place it on her waist.

"Anything you can tell me, you can tell her."

"I'm just trying to make this as easy as possible. I meant nothing by it." I pull lightly on Amy's hand, and she sits back down, more nervous now than ever. She sits with her hands on her lap, fidgeting her fingers.

"I know, Doctor. I just... I hate pushing my loved ones away."

I sit down next to Amy, and she grabs my hand and holds on. I can tell she is worried. Dr Michael nods in agreement and stands up. He grabs a manila folder off his desk and walks his chair over to the area right in front of Amy and me. He sits back down and opens the folder, lays it upon his lap, and begins to speak.

"If you remember at your last check-up I mentioned that the results would take a bit longer because we were getting a new test done."

I nod in agreement and feel Amy tighten her grip. I wonder if keeping her in here is really the best decision. Shouldn't she hear the exact words from me? Either way, it's too late now.

"Well, to put it very briefly, you're going to need surgery. As soon as possible. In fact, we are going to have to admit you tonight. We need to keep you in observation tonight, and we've scheduled you for surgery tomorrow." He rubs his chin and exhales a deep breath. Amy's grip is crushing my fingers.

"Now I already ran it by your parents, and they've approved the operation."

The room is silent, and I say the first thing that comes to my mind.

"Well, surgery tomorrow works for us. We have plans to go see the new *Superman Returns* movie tonight," I say, laughing lightly. I can feel both Amy and Dr Michael staring at me like I'm crazy.

"Rick, you don't understand. If this surgery isn't done soon, you could have a stroke and die. And we need to observe you for eighteen hours before the surgery." The room is silent again, and Amy's grip on my hand loosens.

"And I'm having the surgery tomorrow, right? No big deal."

"We have you scheduled for tomorrow, but we still need to put you under observation." Amy's hand is gone, and her face has gone deadly serious. I lean forward and clench my jaw. Having her here is a bad idea.

"So we could still catch the movie? It's on in an hour or so. We would have plenty of time." I don't know why this movie has suddenly become so important. All I know is that I want to see this movie with Amy. I look over at her, and she has that amazed look again. This whole time, she has been silent. I am now completely regretting keeping her here to hear what the doctor has to say. I didn't think it would be like this.

"Rick, this is serious. Even with the surgery, there is only a fifty percent chance you will make it. The sooner we have it, the better."

"I understand, but if I stay here for four hours or go see a movie, that won't change if I live or die, right?"

He nods reluctantly and closes his manila folder. He stands up, and Amy and I do as well.

"Rick, promise me that you will be back in time," Dr Michael says.

Amy and I move towards the door as I say, "I promise. Just let me have some fun before I have to be cut open and dissected, okay?"

"Okay, just be here in time for the surgery. Your parents will be here by then, and I'll tell them your decision. They'll be...upset, but it's your decision." Dr Michael gestures towards the door, confirming that he is in fact satisfied with this plan.

"Thank you, Doc. Goodbye. I'll see you later tonight." I wave goodbye and reach for Amy's hand, but she's just out of reach.

"How about we catch the movie and have some popcorn and just forget about this whole incident?" I shake my head. "Dr Michael is such a drama queen."

Amy doesn't answer; she just stares at anything but me. We reach the car. I open the door for her and guide her in. Then I run around the back of the car and enter the driver's seat. I have no idea why I'm in such a hurry. Something inside me is pushing me forward, telling me to move quickly, to hurry and not slow down for anything.

I start the car, pull out of the parking lot, and hit the road so fast that the tyres squeal. The inside of the car is quiet; only the soft humming of the tyres and engine can be heard. Lights and buildings streak by, engulfing the car in different light patterns and designs. All too soon, we're sitting in the parking lot of the movie theatre. I look over at Amy. She sits, still as a statue, looking at the dashboard. She has not said a word the whole time.

"Amy...are you all right?"

She slowly turns her head and faces me. She seems to be frustrated and sad.

"Rick, could you take me home?"

"What?" I have heard her, but I don't want to. Something in my head is telling me to go to the theatre. It will be safe there. Nothing can hurt Amy or me while the lights are out and the movie is playing. Everything would be all right if we could just get into the theatre.

"Rick." Amy is louder now, more focused and clear. "Take. Me. Home."

"Are you sure?"

"Yes, I'm sure. Take me home." The words hang in my head, like they have been nailed in there by someone. I turn the car around and head towards Amy's house.

The ride back is silent, empty, and motionless. Neither of us says anything. The radio is on, but the volume is so low that I can only make out snippets of what is playing. We arrive outside her home, and I pull up into the empty driveway. I take a deep breath and turn to face Amy.

"I'm sorry I didn't tell you."

"Tell me what, Rick... that you're going to die?"

"I'm not going to die, Amy. The surgery is going to fix everything."

"The surgery could kill you!"

I'm silent for a while. She does have a point.

"Rick, I really care about you. A lot. But I don't think I can do this."

"Do what?"

"I have so much going on in *my own* life that I can't handle you and the fact that you could very well die tonight. I can't handle that. I can't torture myself with the fact that I am with a guy who doesn't even know his own fate... a guy who doesn't even know if he will see tomorrow."

She is waiting for a response – I can tell by the way she has paused – but for the life of me, I can't figure out what to say. I stare at the steering wheel with my hands at my sides. After a few minutes, Amy seems to decide I'm not going to answer and opens the door. She takes a long look at me and then gets out of the car and closes the door behind her. I don't move till I hear her front door slam behind her.

It takes about five minutes for me to get enough of my brain cells together to do anything. Something is still telling me to go to the theatre, so I head in that direction. I don't notice the tears until I get to the parking lot where Amy and I had just been.

The sounds of people funnelling into the theatre is grating. So many of them are couples; they're holding hands and walking underneath the orange lights. Laughing and smiling, they walk hand in hand. And just like that, rage fills me to the point where I feel like I might explode.

I'm so angry – angry at Amy for leaving me. What does she mean she isn't strong enough? What about me? And why did Dr Michael have to call tonight? Why did I even take that *stupid* test? But the person I'm angry at the most is myself. I should have just told Amy to wait outside. Then we could have gone to the movies, and she would have never known any of this and we would still be together. I slam my fist against the steering wheel so hard that the car alarm goes off. Swallowing my anger, I turn the car back on and head back to the hospital.

Why does my life have to be like this? Why does everyone leave me? Why do I even bother living this wretched life? Who cares how the surgery goes? I'm ready to die, especially if living means that everyone I love will treat me like I'm already dead.

When I get to the hospital, my parents are sitting and talking to each another. The moment they see me, they stand up and rush over to me. I don't tell them about Amy. They've never liked her anyway. They have always thought that she is the one encouraging me to not take my condition seriously. They don't know that I never told her about my condition. The sadness on their faces is so heartbreaking that I don't have it in me to give them bad news anyway. I smile and try to joke around as best as I can. My mom asks me where I went, and I explain I just had to drop Amy off at her house. My mom looks at me with suspicion but doesn't say anything. Even if she has guessed what, it doesn't matter. I'm going to die on the operating table. We move into the prep room, and the nurses surround me like mad scientists with a new experiment. It's not too far from the truth. After all, the next eighteen hours are going to be them 'observing' me, whatever that means.

I spend the rest of the day being hooked up to several different machines and having more blood than I've ever seen in one go taken from me for tests. My mom can barely speak; she fusses over me, fluffing my pillows and patting my head, complaining about the fact that I can't eat before the surgery. My dad sits quietly, speaking only when he can tell that my mom's worrying is starting to get on my nerves. He offers an encouraging word or two before my mom takes the reins again. Finally, I fall asleep.

The next day isn't any better. Doctors and nurses come in and out of my room. They check on the monitors and force smiles, pretending to actually care whether or not I am comfortable. If they really cared, they would let me eat something. I'm so hungry, I could cry. I spend most of the day trying to remember my life before my heart betrayed me, trying to distract myself from how miserable I feel sitting here. I remember running around and playing. I remember being happy. For the first time in a long time, I feel hopeful. If this surgery goes well, then I can go back to that. I'm almost beginning to look forward to the surgery. And finally, after much waiting, it is time for the surgery.

As the nurses poke me with IV needles, a doctor helps put my anaesthesia drip in. I lie quietly, ready to die, to never wake up again. My mom grabs my hand as they wheel me into the OT. Her small hand in mine makes me think of Amy's, and it reminds me of all the things I've lost due to my condition. The small lamp of hope I had earlier today is gone. I close my eyes as we enter the operating room, my last thoughts comprising all the things that this condition has made me lose – the woman I love, my freedom. Deep down I know I'm not coming back alive.

I wake up to the sun's rays falling on my face. I feel weak and tired, and I can barely raise my arms to rub the sleep from my eyes.

"I think he's awake," I hear my mom say while excitedly squeezing my hand.

I hear footsteps quickly cross the room and then my dad's deeper voice. "How are you doing, son?"

I struggle against the drugs to open my eyes and focus on my parents' anxious faces leaning over me. I don't feel any pain, but my head feels like a helium balloon must feel floating near the ceiling, completely disconnected from my body. It takes me a while to remember exactly what happened. "I made it. I actually made it," I say in awe.

Although I have told my parents that I believe everything will be fine, I haven't actually believed I will end up here, alive and fixed. No more worries about my heart. No more pain. I can be a normal person. The relief washes over me, and I have never been so happy. From now on, I am going to take charge of my own life. I'm not sure how, but I am going to get out of their house and actually live this life I have been given. My smile could have lit up a stadium.

"Sweetie, I am so glad you are okay," my mom says as she leans down to give me a hug. It is a little hard to hug though the tubes and wires, but she somehow manages to do it.

At that moment, the intern who often comes in to check on me walks in. "I'm glad to see you are awake. I just have a few tests to make, and then I will go get the doctor for you. Sir, madam, the doctor would like to see you. I just need to do some tests here." My parents glance at each other and thank her before they walk out of the room.

The intern introduces herself as Katy, but I am barely listening. I am still tired after the surgery, and all I can do is watch as she bustles around the bed. Her voice is soft and rhythmic, and soon the effects of it combined with the drugs sends me back to sleep.

I wake up to the sun shining in my face and Katy hanging around the machines.

"Good morning handsome. Are you still hanging around here waiting for me? This is a hospital, not a frat house, you know," she says, smiling at me.

"Really?" I laugh. "It must have been some party for me to end up in the hospital. Too bad I can't remember it. Did I have a good time?"

"How should I know?" she says, faking a pout. "You took off after my shift ended and didn't even bother to invite me. Just like every other boyfriend I've had... leave me alone when the good times roll."

"That's not true. I would never do that to you. How could the good times roll without you?" I say and she blushes.

"Unfortunately so, if I was busy with boyfriends, I wouldn't have time to be here, taking care of people like you. People who fake they are sick just to get waited on hand and foot by the overworked nurses and volunteers."

I laugh. "When the volunteers are as pretty as you, why wouldn't we?"

She blushes again. And I think of the way Amy used to blush and smile when I gave her compliments. I push thoughts of Amy out of my mind and force myself to remember that this is a new life.

"So when do you go home? I'm going to miss you, you know. You're the only cute, young guy in this ward."

Now it's my turn to blush. "I have no idea. From what I hear, I'm going to be here for ten days. But then I get moved to the cardiac ward. Don't suppose you make out-of-ward visits to the sick and lonely, huh?"

"A nice guy like you, lonely? I seriously doubt that. But if you really are that lonely, I might make an exception," she responds.

"Who knows, maybe I'll stop by your house and bring you some more old magazines since you're getting ready to leave this place." I read the numbers out to her.

"Thanks," says Katy. "I might hit you up on the phone and see how you're doing after you get settled in at home. Now how about those tests?"

The few tests consist of drawing blood, reading some of the machines, and checking my bandage.

"You keep pulling out my blood, and my new and improved heart will have nothing to pump," I joked weakly. She laughs as she arranges the drawn blood on her little tray.

"I should take more. That way, you can stay here longer." She glances at her watch and sighs. "I better go before they catch me hanging around here too long."

I nod at her. "As long as you promise to come back often."

"I promise." With a flip of her hair, she turns and leaves the room, leaving behind a hint of perfume.

As she leaves, I settle back into the bed, feeling a sense of happiness and contentment. This new life is going to be perfect.

◎

The next ten days are the most boring of my life. My parents are the only people who are allowed to see me, and even they can only stay for fifteen-minute intervals. The doctors and nurses are frequently waking me up, checking things. Katy stops by whenever she can, even though my parents are constantly there, sometimes right by the bed, sometimes asleep on the couch in the room. Finally, I am able to stay awake for several hours at a time, and the wires and tubes are removed.

"All right, take it easy, we are just going to stand up and walk around the room," the nurse says.

I leap out of bed, glad to be allowed to move. My dad is instantly by my side, laying a big hand on my shoulder and pushing me back onto the bed. "Take it easy, son. You've been through a lot. Your body needs some time."

"I can do this, dad. I am so tired of being in that bed."

"No, honey, listen to your dad, you've been though a lot, and we just want you to take it easy."

"Whatever." I shrug off my dad's hand and stand up again. I place one foot in front of the other and walk around the room slowly. I look right at the doctor and announce, "I am ready to go home."

Despite my demonstration, the doctors still insist that I have to be monitored. I'm moved from the surgical intensive care unit (SICU) to the cardiac unit, which is better since I'm given a private room and can receive more guests. But it's also worse because I have to be trapped there for a whole month.

The days drag by like snails. I spend my time planning out my future, now that I have one again. Katy and Jacob stop by when they can, and my parents are never gone for very long. The nurses joke that they may need to get my mom a closet so she can just move in, she's here so much. Still, I count the days till I will be free again.

Months later, I'm back to my life again. It's strange. Everyone treats me the same way, despite the fact that I've been through this massive change in my life. Even though I was bedridden for three months, the world kept spinning while I was out of the loop. While I was lying on an operating table, people were making new friends; new couples were getting together. Even Jacob is a little different. He seems more mature now than he did before; he even has a girlfriend now.

The only thing that hasn't changed is my parents. They still worry too much, saying that I am doing too much too fast, but I love the feeling of movement without pain way too much. I never want to sit still again.

I'm at a party one day, sitting next to Jacob and sipping on my drink, when Amy and her new boyfriend walk by us. Girls like her don't stay single for long. She avoids me now, acting like we are strangers.

"Why did you guys break up? I thought things were doing great."

"Me too, just goes to show you never know."

"What happened?"

"Well, she learned I was on the verge of death and decided she needed someone *without* one foot in the grave," I answer bitterly.

"Come on, she didn't."

"Yeah, she did, right before surgery. I thought we were meant to be together."

"Just goes to show, beauty really is only skin deep. She's not good enough for you. At least you saw her true side before you went to college together. Who needs someone like that? Just wait, you are going to meet some girl who is beautiful inside and out."

"This touching moment brought to you by Hallmark," I joke.

"Speaking of beautiful inside and out... whatever happened to Katy?"

I smile. Thinking of Katy always brings a smile to my face. Even though her family had to move because her dad got a new job, we still talk all the time.

"Well, her dad got a job in..."

The rest of the year passes by in a blur of social outings, and finally, I feel like I have a place in the world again. Step 1 of my 'new life' plan is complete, and step 2 is well underway. For weeks, I've been scanning the newspapers, looking for a job and applying for all the ones that I can do. I've even had a few interviews. Even though I have a few options, I am holding out for the perfect job. It is perfect; it is a morning shift watching security monitors. No manual labour, and afternoon's free for hanging out. It doesn't really pay much, but in my family, money's never been a problem. I know that I can get a job in the family business, but I'd much rather work where people won't treat me like the boss's son. I'm thinking of all the things I'll do if I get the job when my phone rings.

"Hello."

A woman's voice comes on. "Hi, is this Rick?"

"Yes, it is."

"Rick, this is Michelle from human resources at Millingsway Security. You interviewed with us last week. I just wanted to let you know you've got the position."

"I have?" My skin almost bursts.

"Yes, can you be here on Monday at 8 a.m. for orientation?"

"Of course!"

"Good. Congratulations!"

"Thank you."

I run down the stairs, almost bursting with my good news. "Mom, guess what?"

She looked up with horror on her face. "Rick, how many times have I told you, you *cannot* run?"

I am too excited to pay attention; besides, I've never felt better. "Mom... guess what!" Without waiting for an answer I cry out, "I got a job, I start Monday."

"What? When? You don't need a job. We will get everything you need for you."

"That's just it, Mom. I am sick of depending on you for everything. I want to start doing things for myself."

"We'll talk about this when your dad gets home from work."

I shrug off her lack of enthusiasm; Dad will support me in this anyway. He's always talking about how a man has to be responsible.

That night at dinner, I excitedly tell Dad about the new job. The look on his face is murderous. "What?" he sputters. "Why would you do something like that?"

'Dad, I am seventeen now. I am tired of not being able to do anything. It is not like I am out getting drunk or something. I am trying to get a job and be responsible like you always say. I don't see what the big deal is. Besides, you haven't even heard what it is."

"It doesn't matter. You don't need to be doing anything that might hurt you. If you want a job so badly, you can work with us. It's about time you started to learn about the family business."

I feel a surge of happiness. My dad has never tried to bring me into the family business. I always felt like he thought it would be a waste of time. I know my father loves me, but I've always had the feeling that he's been waiting for me to die. Letting me join the family business means that he finally has faith in my ability. If I had known he wanted me in the business, I would never have looked for another job.

"That's a brilliant idea!" My mom joins in. "Then we know that someone can always keep an eye on you if you ever feel bad."

My heart sinks. I realize that this is just another way for them to 'monitor' me.

"I feel fine," I mumble, but I know that arguing is pointless.

When Monday rolls around, I get into the car with my father, hoping that the feeling I have in the pit of my stomach is wrong.

The next few weeks are everything I was dreading. I am never allowed to do any work, and I am constantly being 'checked on'. I spend my time on the Internet, looking up new and interesting things about the university that I am going to be attending in the next few months.

I've been chatting online with a few of my friends who are going to be in the same classes. It's going to be great being away from the house even if it's just for a few months. I'm checking my email for what seems like the billionth time today when my phone rings.

"Hello, may I speak to Rick?"

"This is Rick."

"Rick, this is John. I'm your guidance counsellor here at the university. I just wanted to confirm that you are switching your classes to correspondence."

"Correspondence classes…?"

"Yes, our correspondence courses allow you to take your classes from the comfort of your home. We were informed of your health condition, and we want to make sure that you can get your degree without risking your health."

I freeze; the knowledge that my parents have done this behind my back is astounding.

"Rick…Rick…are you there?"

"Yes, I'm here. John, can I call you back?"

"Of course."

I hang up the phone, livid. I head straight to my father's office, closing the door behind me with a click. He looks up at me, and the look on my face must have told him something. He waves away the secretary who is holding a stack of papers for him to sign. As soon as she leaves the room, I say as evenly as I can manage.

"Did you know about the correspondence courses?"

He sighs softly. "Your mom thinks it would be a good idea. That way, you can get your degree, and we can keep an eye on you."

'An eye on me! When are you guys going to stop treating me like some damaged child? You're constantly stopping me from living a full life. I'm so done!"

I stomp out of the room, heading for my car and speeding all the way home.

My mom is sitting in the kitchen, reading a paper as if nothing is wrong. How can she ruin my life like this and not even care? I walk past her into the living room and grab a vase that she's had for years and slam it to the floor. Now she'll know what it feels like to lose something she loves. I head to my room and fall into the bed.

A few minutes later, my mom comes in. "Rick, what was that about?"

"As if you don't know? You guys are destroying my life. You won't let me do anything. All I want is to be normal."

"Sweetie," she begins with a sigh.

"Don't... just don't. I don't want to see you or talk to you." I roll over, pulling the covers over my head. I reach for my headphones and turn the music up as loud as it would go. I never want to hear her voice again. My heart is beating so hard, it hurts against my chest. I close my eyes and ignore it.

For the next week, my parents and I barely talk. They try to bribe me by letting me hang out with Jacob and buying me things. And after a while, it works. The pain that I had after our big argument keeps coming back, but there is no way I am going to tell my parents about it. If they knew about the pain, they would never let me out of the house. I'm not going to lose the precious little freedom I have left in my life. They still let me spend some time with Jacob, and if I would lose that, then I would go crazy. If I would tell them about the new chest pains, they would treat me even worse. As it is, I'm treated like I'm broken and damaged, like a bird with a broken wing in a cage.

One night I'm lying in bed, trying to figure out how to convince my parents to let me go to the beach tomorrow with Jacob, when a sharp pain catches me. The pain is so bad, I can't hide the scream as I clutch my chest. I gasp for breath, rolling around and trying to find a position that will help. But nothing works and I fall off the bed.

That is how my parents find me, writhing around on the floor, clutching my chest and crying. I barely notice as my dad scoops me and heads to the car. The world is a blur around me, and I fade in and out of consciousness.

I barely remember the ride to the hospital. People are swarming around me, asking me questions or sticking things into me. I barely even notice. The pain is excruciating.

Soon the doctors figure everything out and do something to ease the pain. When they are done with their poking and prodding, they leave me and my parents alone.

"I am so sorry, I should have told you—" I say softly.

"That's right. You should have told us," my dad cuts in. "What were you thinking?"

"Maybe if you wouldn't treat me like a rat in a cage..." I begin, my temper starting to flare.

I am interrupted by the doctor who has a sombre expression on his face. "I am afraid I have some bad news. We have found two more blockages that were missed in the last surgery. He needs to go back into surgery..."

"What!" my father yells. He's angrier than I have ever seen him. "You said the surgery will cure him. Now you tell me you *missed* some blockages! How do you miss blockages?"

"Sir...please try to understand..."

"Understand, *understand*! You stand there and tell me that my son's life is in danger for the second time in six months, and you expect me to *understand*? For as much money as we are paying at this hospital!"

"Dad."

"I will sue you. This kind of mistake will not be tolerated."

"Dad."

"You will never work in this tow—"

"Dad!"

He stops to look at me as if he had forgotten we were all there.

"I'm going to be fine. These things are complicated, right Doctor?"

I glance at him while he nods anxiously. The fear of getting sued by someone as influential as my father is enough to put fear into his heart. I smile at them both.

"He's just trying to do his job. And I don't think yelling at the man in charge of cutting me up is going to help much."

My dad looks from the doctor to me, and I can see his anger being put away. He realizes that I'm right.

"Now, Doctor, what are the risks involved?" I ask.

At this point, the doctor seems hesitant, and I prepare myself for bad news.

"Well...umm... Due to the fact that we are doing another surgery so soon after the last one, the risks are high. The chance of survival is... about... about ten percent."

My mom bursts into tears, and the only sound in the room is the sound of her sobs. My heart sinks. For the second time in less than a year, I accept the fact that my life is over.

The drive home from the hospital after I have been released is quiet. My father is still stewing, mad at not just me but the hospital as well. Despite what I said at the hospital, I feel the same way he does. That surgery was supposed to cure me! I can feel the anger well up in my chest, and I hold on to it. I glance at both my parents. They are both healthy. What did I do that was so wrong? How come I'm the only person suffering this way. Will I ever be able to have a normal life? I stare out into the road and watch people walking down the street. Some are bustling around, trying to get on with their daily lives. Others are holding hands and smiling, couples are on dates, and children are playing. Will I ever be able to go and enjoy life as these people are, or will I be forever trapped in the cage that my condition has created for me?

I spend the next few days sitting at home, watching TV, or messing around on the Internet. Nothing seems important anymore. After all, what's the point of doing anything when you're waiting to die? Today I'm out watching people as they come in and out of the cafe I've decided to have lunch in. I've become obsessed with watching other people live the life I want so badly. I sometimes imagine myself in their position, making up a fantasy life to replace the miserable one that I have. For example, there's a couple in the corner who are acting like they belong in some movie. They are all blushes and smiles as they share their plate of fries.

I imagine myself in his place, giggling, laughing, and being happy. And for a few moments, I can escape the pain. In my fantasy, it is me putting an arm around her, and the laughter trickling from her throat is at something I have said. She tucks a strand of her hair behind her ear and bats her eyelashes at me in that flirtatious move that girls do so well to drive men crazy. The waiter stops by our table and interrupts us, asking if we would like anything else. I'm annoyed that he is interrupting this perfect moment, but I smile at him, knowing that getting annoyed will not win me any points with the wonderful girl by my side. I turn to her and ask her if she needs anything. She shakes her head and mentions that it is getting late and she needs to get back to work. I glance at my watch and realize that I am also late. I tell her that being with her eliminates the concept of time. She blushes again, and we stand up to leave.

The motion breaks the fantasy that I was so pleasantly building. It is not me enjoying a lunch break. Such simple pleasures are not for the likes of me. I frown. Why can't I just be normal? Why am I so different? I glance at the door that the couple has just gone through, wondering where they are going. When the waiter comes to ask me if I want anything else, I ask for a beer. When it comes, I let the cool taste slide over my tongue. This is one thing I can do like the rest of the world. I can drown away my sorrows.

After an hour, I've had at least six beers, and I am feeling... not good... never that. I am numb, and the numbness is better than the pain of knowing that I can't have a full life. I pick myself up, slam enough to cover my bill and a generous tip to the waiter for having to handle waiting on such a pathetic excuse of a human being, and leave. Surely, there must be a bar around here that won't mind having some of my money without giving me worried looks.

Over the next few weeks, I develop a pattern. I would go out in public and observe other people going about their lives. I would look at them as closely as I could, trying to think what they were thinking – and preferably what they were thinking of me. I would try to read their thoughts, like a fortune-teller holding out her hands. Yet in my envy, I would judge them. In my mind, I would criticize and memorize their moves and behaviour, the curves of their bodies, the grooves on their faces – whichever it was that caught my eye. I would look at them and try to figure out what it was about them that made them worthy of happiness.

I was so enveloped in their looks, their skin, their hair, and their eyes that I could barely take my own eyes off them. I would gaze deep into a scar on a cheek, a pimple or dimple on a face, and I would think, *What makes you different from me? Why do you have blue eyes – as blue as the sky and sea – and I have brown?* Envy of others' lives would eat at me.

I would gaze at people as they walked down the street, fascinated with even the simplest of things. I was entranced with the curling locks of redheads, the pin-straight blondes, the wavy hair of brunettes, and the short crops of professionals. I was so obsessed that I forgot what my own hair looked like until I would catch a glance in a mirror or dark window that reflected my figure.

Figures were another thing in itself. My jealous jade eyes would catch a glimpse of a beautifully slender woman and I would think to myself, *How do you deal with bestowing such beauty? What is your life like as a lifelike doll – with the body of a model?*

My obsession with people didn't end with the beautiful. I would see a portly older person, a man perhaps of middle age buying a pack of cigarettes, and I would watch him as he'd laugh at the clerk as he'd pass him the smokes and wonder in envy of his high spirits – high spirits that were the total opposite of his physical appearance.

I would marvel at a mentally challenged man with his mom shopping at a grocery store, looking and touching and feeling all the colourful fruits at the produce department. It was as if that was his first time ever seeing an apple or pear. I was jealous of his childlike behaviour when he was a grown man on the outside. His mother would snap at him and tell him to stop touching the fruit, to not make a scene. Yet no one was really paying attention, except me.

In my own little weird way, I wanted to act the same way. I wanted to act like him and touch all the beautiful and bountiful fruit like it was my first time too. I watched him and envied his freedom to do whatever he pleased. I wished I could have that freedom; after all, society deemed us both damaged. How did his damage make him free and mine brought me a cage?

To me, everyone I saw was beautiful. As long as they were able to live the life they chose, I would find beauty in them. There was beauty in their freedom. And in myself, I could only see the ugliness of a trapped and damaged man.

There was only one way to get rid of the ugliness, and that was to drown myself in alcohol. Although my days were filled with careful introspection and analysis, my nights were a blur. I'd stop by a bar and order a drink, and I wouldn't stop until all the money I came with was gone. At the bar, I could be the life of the party. I would offer anyone that took an interest in me a drink and use the lubrication to ask all the questions that would plague me during the day but I could not ask. They would respond as well and as politely as they could. All the while, their eyes shining with pity. Sooner or later, they would not be able to take the questions and would excuse themselves.

At that point, I would head back home, slipping in to avoid my parents' watchful gaze. I would crash on the bed and enjoy the happiest point of my day. The numbness would take over, and right before I passed out, I would think, *Wouldn't it be better to just die?*

As the days pass, I isolate myself from people more and more. Although I spend a lot of my time around people, I will not allow anyone into the inner workings of my heart. My family and friends are completely oblivious of the way I am feeling. I prefer them not to be stained with my damage. It is bad enough that they have had to deal with all the ups and downs of my life. So I build a wall around myself and will let no one pass through.

The person that comes closest to breaking my wall is Jacob. Although he is busy with his own life now, what with Susan (his girlfriend) and his new job, he still somehow finds the time to hang out with his degenerate friend. He is constantly calling me and asking how I am. About once a week, he makes sure to spend time with me. Although I know he is just trying to be a good friend, I can only see his constant attention as an indication of pity. If I were normal, he wouldn't be doing this.

Today he has decided that I *must* come out with him and Susan. Apparently, there's some big party going on that I must attend. I agree to go reluctantly. The only reason to accept is the fact that the party is being hosted at a bar. And I know that among all the drunken merriment, I will fit right in.

When Jacob comes to get me (he's realized I won't show up if he doesn't), Susan is already with him. She jumps out of the car and bounds towards me with a hug and a smile.

"Rick! It's so good to see you. I haven't seen you in ages. Where have you been?"

I smile back. Susan is one of those genuinely nice people. She always has a smile for everyone. And she genuinely cares about people. She is going to make a great nurse someday.

"Oh, just here and there," I respond, "trying to recover from losing my best friend to the most amazing girl in the world." She laughs at this.

"Don't worry, if Jacob pisses me off enough, I'll have to return him to you." We both laugh, and then her face turns serious. She grabs my arm and leans in to whisper.

"Don't be mad, but Jacob told me about the surgery. I just wanted to let you know that I'm sorry and that if you ever need to talk, Jacob and I are here for you. I might not be the smartest person in the world, but my shoulders are great for leaning on."

I want to get angry, but the sincerity in her eyes is too real for me to be anything but touched. For a second, I feel her compassion.

"Thank you, Susan."

She smiles happy at her good deed. Then she ruins it by saying, "I'll be praying for you."

That makes me angry. If prayers work, my mom has done enough praying to build me a new heart. The sarcasm in my voice is acidic.

"Yeah... maybe he'll listen to you this time," I say. And I see her face fall right before I turn and head to the car. I feel bad for hurting her, but right now, the last thing I want to hear is about god's miracles. He's the reason I'm in this mess in the first place.

I get into the car, and Jacob throws me a questioning look. I shrug, and he turns to Susan as she gets into the car as well. She turns to smile at me.

"It's really nice that you could come, Rick," she says in that sincere voice of hers, and instantly, I feel like an ass. It's not her fault that my life is crap.

"Thanks, it's always a pleasure hanging out with you."

I know she'll understand that this is my way of apologizing to her. I would actually say the words, but I can't without letting Jacob know that I'm being such a louse to his girlfriend. He glances at the two of us but decides to let it go, and we head out into the night.

The bar is loud and noisy when we get there. Several people are already well on their way to being drunk, and I smile. In this crowd, I'll blend right in.

A week later, I'm sitting at home, fresh from the hospital. I'd had another attack today, and right now, I'm more tired than I have ever been in my life. The moon is high in the sky, as if mocking me. Its Cheshire cat grin is a reminder of all the smiles that I have missed. I sit at the desk in my room, pulling a pen and paper to write my thoughts.

I pick up the pen, trying to fill in the blank whiteness with words and thoughts that I have never confessed. Images of bitter and sweet moments that belong only to me flash in my head. I try to think of a time when I was happy. I can't believe it's so hard to remember. I had a life once, but it seems so long ago. It feels like a jagged memory. Like remembering a dream someone else had. I think instead of the pain. Surely, I can write about that. The pain that is with me every waking moment, surely I can express that. I place the pen to paper and begin to write.

I called to you, Mr Death, when I was only eleven.
Why didn't you take me? Didn't I deserve heaven?
By then, hadn't I suffered enough?
Why are you making my life so tough?
Why won't you come, take me away from this lie?
Why won't you give me peace and just let me die?
Please, Mr Death, I'm begging you to come
And take me back to wherever I'm from.
I don't belong here, shunned by my race.
Can't you see the pain in my face?
I'm being blamed, but I have no control.
My life is already over – I live six feet in a hole.

Words are pouring out of me. As time goes by, I find myself listening only to the rhythmic cracking of my knuckles.

Please, Mr Death, I'm begging you to come
I need to go back to wherever I'm from
I'm being buried alive – my life I can't save
I'm dying inside; let me lie in my grave.
Can't you see it's too unbearable for me?
Why won't you come and set my mind free?
Please, Mr Death, I'm begging you to come
I hate myself for what I have become.
People here will never accept who I am.
Why should they? They just don't give a damn.
They say my feelings are one and theirs are many.
What does this mean? That I shouldn't have any?
Papers forced into balls of different shapes are scattered
over the floor like tiles.
Please, Mr Death, if you don't come soon,
I'm afraid I'll be locked up in some padded room.

I'm losing my mind, and I can't hold it together.
I feel a bone numbing cold like the severest of weather.
My mind and body will soon succumb to this pain.
I won't be able to stop myself from going insane.
Please, Mr Death, I promise I won't hide.
I can't fill this emptiness I have deep inside.
Why didn't you take me so long ago?
I had my bags packed; I was ready to go.
You let me feel peace – something I lack.
Then you played a cruel trick and sent me back.
Please, Mr Death, you've had your fun.
Now why don't you come back and get the job done?
I'm getting so tired of living this life.
Haven't you laughed hard enough watching me cry?
Oh please, Mr Death, I'm begging you to find
The time to take my soul and ease my weary mind.

I am flooded by annoyance at my lack of words and literary incompetence. As despair flows through me, I head to the bathroom; my throat is ragged from sobs. In the bathroom, I find the glass that is always there for me. Right next to it are the pills from the hospital that they give me to fight off the pain.

I laugh bitterly at them. Painkillers! How have they helped me with pain? Here I am dying inside, and they sit there quietly mocking me. Then a thought occurs to me. Maybe they can help. Maybe I just haven't been taking enough.

I reach for the bottle and place a few in my palm. Their whiteness contrasts against my skin in the moonlight. I swallow them slowly and feel nothing but them sliding down my throat. The pain is still there. I take a few more. Still nothing. Even more and no response. The pain is still there.

I head back to my room and begin to type up an email to Jacob. Maybe if I let him in, he can help me, since god has so clearly forsaken me.

When I am done, I read through and sigh. Even in this, I have failed. I turn off the computer and head back to the bathroom. I down what is left of the pills and head to bed. Surely, I have had enough to end this pain. Surely, the painkillers will do their job and end the pain, permanently.

Jacob

"Come on. Come on," I snarl at the car in front of me. He is going the speed limit, but it feels way too slow. I am going to go insane. His blinker flashes, and he slows down to turn into the parking lot. I step on the gas, swing wide, and pass him.

A part of me screams a warning, "Slow down, you will just get pulled over." I can't help it though. I have to hurry. Usually, I am a safe driver. I grip the steering wheel and grind my teeth. The stop light is red. As I wait, I tap my fingers impatiently and think back to fifteen minutes ago. Back when life was great.

It began like any other morning. I was in bed, having a great dream when 'My heart will go onnnnnn...' interrupted my sleep.

"Ugh." I rolled over and hit the alarm, ending the dreadful noise. Why did it always seem like morning came too soon? The sun's rays filtered though the blinds, promising yet another beautiful and warm fall day. It should have been getting colder, but this summer just seemed to stretch on forever. I yawned and sat up, taking a deep breath. That was a mistake. The air smelled of burnt toast and eggs. I have never met someone as incompetent in the kitchen as my roommate. The guy could burn water.

I picked up my phone to check my emails and the weather for the day. It was going to be warm (no surprise there). Maybe Rick and I could go hang out at the park today. Susan, my girlfriend, and I were thinking about doing a BBQ soon. Today would probably be a great day for it. Rick must have been thinking the same thing. I had an email from him. I clicked on it and started reading. That is when the day started to go downhill.

"Jacob," I read. "I cannot live this life anymore. I cannot live from one surgery to the next, never knowing if I will wake up on the other side. This new surgery gives me a ninety percent chance of dying. I would rather die on my own terms. I don't want to be dissected and then never get put back together. I am tired of living a life where I cannot do anything active, where walking to the bus stop could kill me. I am tired of it all. Thanks for being such a great friend. I knew I could always count on you. I wish things could be different. Thanks for everything. I am sorry for all the pain I have caused you and will cause you. Please forgive me. Please help my parents to understand. Your friend, Rick."

I had to read it twice before it sunk in. He was going to kill himself. I jumped out of bed. I had to get there. Maybe I wasn't too late. I grabbed some clothes and hastily threw them on. Why is it that whenever you are in a hurry you cannot get dressed fast enough? In my rush, I put my shirt on backwards and got my feet tangled up in my pant legs. I slid my feet into my shoes. I hopped around, trying to tie the laces. I grabbed my phone and keys with one hand while opening the front door with the other.

"Jacob! You want some eggs?" my roommate called after me, holding up the skillet proudly.

"I have to go now!" I said running down the hall and wrinkling my nose at the idea of eating those eggs. I pushed the button for the elevator, but it was too slow. Instead, I ran down the stairs, skipping several at a time. My feet echoed in the stairwell and seemed to keep pace with my thoughts. "Faster...Faster..." they thudded. When I was near the bottom, I just swung over the railing and skipped the last five altogether. I threw open the door, banging it against the wall, and rushed out into the bright sunlight. Squinting, I jammed the key into the lock and got into the car. I threw it in reverse and left the parking lot in a shower of smoke and squealing noises.

The light finally changes, and I shoot ahead. Soon, I am on the freeway. I slide into traffic and settle in for the ride. On a good day, it takes about twenty minutes to go from my dorm room on campus to Rick's home in the suburbs. However, it is rush hour, and the trip will last at least twice that long. That means I have forty long minutes before I learn if my best friend is still alive.

I still don't really understand it. I thought Rick was doing better. I know he thought things weren't that great, but it seemed like he had been laughing and joking around a lot more. Just last week, we had gone to the beach together. He had gotten super drunk with the rest of us. We had stayed up until dawn, singing songs around the bonfire on the beach. It had been great, at least until the hangover. But we had been having a lot of fun. Where were the signs that things weren't going well? I guess there was the fact he started taking correspondence classes when all he had talked about was how great it was going to be to live on campus. "I am just going to learn the family business," he had said. At the time, I had accepted it as truth, but now I wondered. Then there were his jokes. Rick had always been so upbeat and positive. You could always count on him to have a joke or a good story. Lately, though, his jokes had seemed a little more forced and his laughs a little more bitter. Maybe I should have seen this coming. We had talked a little about the upcoming surgery. I knew he was worried. I also knew that he would frequently get drunk, but I just thought it was his way of dealing with his parents' oppressive hold on him. Maybe I had been wrong. I should have seen this coming. I should have been there for him. I should have hung out with him more instead of going out with Susan. I should have called him.

"Called him! That's it!" I shout out loud.

I pull out my phone and hit the speed dial. Number 3, Rick. Maybe I could talk him out of it before it is too late. The phone starts ringing. "One, two, three," I mentally count, "four, five…"

"Hello…"

"Rick!" I shout into the receiver.

"This is Rick's phone. Rick and I are playing hide-and-seek right now. If you leave a message, I will tell him as soon as he finds me. Have a great day. Bye. Please leave a message after the beep."

I hit the end-call button on my phone. Hard. "Please, oh please, don't let me be too late," I pray. It has been a long time since I have prayed. My parents used to take me to the temple every Saturday, but since I moved out, I have stopped going. Hopefully, god does not hold grudges.

I step on the brake and squeal to a stop outside Rick's home. I am going to need new tyres after today. I run up the steps and pound on the door. I bounce on the balls of my feet, waiting. Finally, Rick's mom opens the door.

"Jacob, we weren't expecting you today. What brings you here so early in the morning?"

"Where's Rick?" I ask craning my neck to see around her into the dining room. Rick's dad is calmly eating breakfast while reading the morning edition of the paper. I cannot see Rick. "Where's Rick?" I repeat.

"He is upstairs, asleep," his mom answers, opening the door a little wider for me even as she frowns in disapproval of my rushed state. "Why don't you go wake him up?"

I step inside and head for the stairs. "Just a minute, son," Rick's dad says. I hesitate, one foot on the stairs. "Is everything okay? You seem a little rushed."

"Umm, yeah. Everything is okay," I say, hoping it is true.

"Hmm…"

I haven't heard the rest as I am already throwing open Rick's door.

Inside the room, it is quiet and dim. Rick is lying on his bed, facing the wall. I run to him and shake him. "Rick, Rick," I say helplessly.

"Whoa! Whoa! What are you doing, trying to shake my head off?" Rick barks sleepily.

I jump back, falling on my butt in the middle of the room. Rick, who I have thought is dead, sits up and stretches lazily. I jump up and hug him.

"What's wrong with you?" he says, eyeing me suspiciously.

"You sent me an email. You said…" I stop. I cannot get the words out.

"Oh."

"That is all you can say? 'Oh.' I thought you were gone. I practically flew over here."

"I guess you got my email. I didn't mean to send it."

"Well, you did. You have a lot of explaining to do, man. And this time, no lying or beating around the bush."

Rick starts talking. Once he is able to start, nothing can stop him. He tells me that he has actually tried to kill himself, but it has not worked. He has lain in bed awake all night, trying to figure out why he can't just die.

"My entire life, I have lived like I would die at any given moment, but then when I try to die, I can't." Rick laughs bitterly. "I hate knowing that I will never have a life, that I will never be normal. I hate the pain, the almost constant pain I have to live with."

We talk for almost an hour about the miserable situation. Then we are quiet.

"What now?" I ask.

"I don't know."

"Come with me," I say. I suddenly know where Rick needs to go. I leave the room so he can get dressed, and then we head downstairs.

"Everything okay, boys?" Rick's mom enquires as we head out of the door.

"Sure, everything is just fine," I reassure her. "I just want to show Rick something."

We drive to the temple that I've been visiting since my childhood. It is beautiful. Its spires reach to heaven; the carvings depict ancient holy symbols. The grounds are lush with flowers and exotic trees. We step inside, and a warm peace envelops us. It is dark compared to outside, and we wait for our eyes to adjust before slipping on to a cold, hard bench. I stare up at the statues and paintings that hang on the wall. I remember being enthralled with them as a child. "I used to come here every week with my parents," I whisper in the solemn silence. "I think this is the best place to try and put your life back together."

Rick nods silently. Then tears start to flow down his face. "I want to do better, I *will* do better," he says. Together we come up with a plan.

"I want to know exactly what you are going to do," I encourage him.

"Well, I am going to stop trying to take my life," Rick says. I look hard at him, and he stares back. "Seriously," he says. "Oh, and I won't go to bars anymore."

'What about the future?'

"It just seems so pointless. I might not even survive this surgery."

"At least it will give you something to plan on, a reason to fight through and not give up. They say that people overcome worse odds if they have something worth living for," I encourage him. "Maybe you can start doing more at work."

Rick throws me a dirty look. "You know my father will never allow that."

"Yeah...but he can't stop you from doing things he doesn't know about," I say, trying to appeal to Rick's cheeky side.

He smiles and says, "That *is* true."

The smile encourages me, and I press on, "And I'm sure that with your brains, you can become invaluable to the company really quickly. That way, when your dad finds out, he'll realize the truth about you."

He stares at me suspiciously. "The truth?"

"That you're an awesome guy with lots of potential."

He smiles again. "Okay, so no more bars or death attempts, and I am going to actually work at work," Rick says, and I can see a hint of his former smile. "Now why did you bring me here of all the places we could have gone?"

"This is where I feel closest to god," I reply. "This is where I can pray without feeling out of place. I think you need to pray for help. I also think you need to pray for peace and hope."

"Okay." Rick closes his eyes and then opens them again. "I don't know if I know how to do this anymore."

"It is easy. Just talk to him as if he were sitting beside you. I will say it if you want." Rick nods. I take a deep breath, willing the butterflies out of my belly. It suddenly occurs to me just how long it has been since my last real prayer. I feel Rick's eyes on me, waiting. I begin. I like to say it is a wonderful, inspired prayer, but it isn't. It is a very short but very heartfelt prayer. I pray that Rick will treasure the life he has been given and that he will have the strength to live his life and overcome the pain. "Amen," I say quietly at the end.

"Amen," Rick agrees.

We sit for some time on the benches, lost in our thoughts. I watch the dust motes float lazily in the sunlight, streaming in the windows. I think of how close I have been to losing my best friend and how lucky I am that I did not.

Finally, we stand up to leave. As we rise, Rick says, "Thanks. You will never understand what you have done for me. I feel hope again. The next time I come here, I want to bring my true love."

I look at him and laugh. "Oh yeah? And who would the lucky lady be? Did you pick up on a girl at all these bars you've been going to?"

"No," Rick says, punching me on the arm. "I don't know her yet, but when I do meet her, I want to show her this," he says, waving his arm, and I know exactly what he means.

Rick

It is Wednesday night. I am sitting alone at home, slouched on the couch, watching something on TV. My parents are out tonight, and I have a brief reprieve from their watchful eyes. They don't say much anymore, but their worry is almost palpable. It is nice to be alone for once. They have invited me to go with them, but it is some business dinner, and I really don't want to go out and sit stiffly with a bunch of businessmen who are trying to one-up one another without looking too pretentious. So here I sit. I don't really want to be here either. I think about going to the park, but the thought of watching children experience the carefree childhood I never had is almost as repulsive to me as the business dinner. Only one place sounds good to me right now. I close my eyes and imagine the feeling of a cold beer sliding down my throat. It will only take a few before the buzz will kill this anguish. I rise to get my car keys. I am going to go. Suddenly Jacob's face replaces the cold glass in my mind. I remember the promise I made to him just days ago. I promised to not drink so much and to do something with my life. No matter how long that life might be. It is just so hard. Why is it that good habits are so easy to break and bad ones so hard? If you miss one day of eating a healthy breakfast, the next day you don't even remember that you have been trying to eat well. However, if you miss a day of going to the bar, the next day you want to go twice as bad.

I flop back into the couch and cover my face with my hands. "What am I going to do?" I moan. "This is too hard." Then I remember. I can go back to the temple Jacob showed me. I felt at peace there; I felt could get my life back. As soon as I think about the temple, I know there is only one place I want to be right now, and I need to get there fast. I jump up, throw on a light sweater, and jog out to the car.

I sit in the temple parking lot. Now that I am here, I am afraid to go in. What if it is not the same? I watch a couple stroll up the pathway hand in hand. Although it is getting dark, I can see their faces in the street light. She spontaneously turns and gives him a kiss on the cheek. I can hear her light laugh even in the car. They look so happy together. I wonder again if anyone would ever feel that way about me. Then I remember that I have told Jacob that the next time I am here I want to bring my true love. Oh well, if I don't make it through the next surgery, I am not going to find true love, and right now, I really need the peace of the temple. I take a deep breath and get out of the car.

Inside the temple, it is warm and quiet. Once again, I feel that serene feeling envelop me. I am immediately at peace. I sink into a bench and just sit quietly, trying to figure out my life. I close my eyes and start talking to god. I am not as good at it as Jacob, but I figure if he is as loving as I have been told, he will overlook this.

"Please, god," I whisper, "I don't know what to do. I am so scared. The doctor says I can die without the surgery. But he also says if I have the surgery, I might die anyway. I don't want to die." I pause for a moment, tears streaming down my face. The fear in me is overwhelming. It has just occurred to me that dying means I will live in heaven with him. And even that thought doesn't cheer me up. There's so much stuff I want to do in this life. I'm not ready to go to the next. Not yet.

"I hope I didn't offend you. It is not the idea of living in heaven with you that I mind," I try to amend. "I just want to be able to live this life here and now. There are so many things I want to do. If I will live through this surgery, please help it to happen quickly so I can try to pick up the pieces of my life. Please help me to live. Please help me to live. Please help me to..."

At that moment, my phone starts vibrating in my pocket. I try to ignore it, but it keeps shaking insistently. I pull it out and look at the caller's name – Dr Michael. It takes a few moments for me to fully realize why he would be calling. "Hello," I say shakily, wiping my tears away.

"Hi, Rick, this is Dr Michael."

"Yes?" I hesitate. It is never good news when your doctor calls you.

"I have some good news for you. Do you think you and your parents could stop by the office some time tomorrow?"

"Does this mean I am better?" I joke, knowing that I am not. My heart has been hurting a lot lately.

"No, but we are ready for surgery. Why don't we wait until tomorrow to talk about the details in person? How is 9.30?"

"That sounds great," I say, trying to keep the fear out of my voice. "See you tomorrow."

I hang up. I am going to have a surgery. I am scared; this is it. I try to remember what I was doing before the call. Through the fogginess of fear, I remember I was praying that I would live. The realization makes me sit up straight. God heard me. He heard me and answered my prayer. I am going to have this surgery, and I am going to live. For the first time in a long time, I feel joy. I want to run down the aisle and jump in the moonlight, but I know that isn't possible. After all, I want to live long enough to have the surgery.

Thursday morning is cloudy and drizzly. However, I am on top of the world. I have had a sign that god wants me to live. My parents and I drive in silence to the hospital and sit in the waiting room. It still smells like a hospital – that mix of sick and bleach. The room is painted in sickly green. I am sure it is meant to be soothing, but I never would have painted a room that colour. It makes you nauseous just looking at it. I thumb through a magazine while we wait for Dr Michael. I cannot focus on the words though. I bounce my knees and try not to think of the upcoming meeting.

After about five minutes of waiting, my name is called. We all stand up as if we have been sitting on fire. We follow the cute nurse in a single file down the hall to the doctor's office. This room is familiar to me. I have been here way too many times. We take our usual seats and commence without any small talk.

"I believe we are ready to do the surgery," Dr Michael states.

"We are too."

"Before we get to the surgery though, there are a few things we need to talk about. As I have said before, this is a very high-risk surgery. The odds of Rick making it through are ten percent. However, if he does make it though, the quality of his life will greatly improve."

I swallow nervously. Ten percent odds I wake up on the other side. The thought is chilling. Then I remember I have a sign. I will wake up.

"Let's get it done," I say.

"Not so fast," Dr Michael says. "Before we do this surgery, we want to observe you for two weeks. We need to know you are in the best condition possible."

"Two weeks is a long time," my dad voices my thoughts. "Does that entire time have to be here?"

"I am afraid so. We can begin right away, or you can go home and get things settled first. It is entirely up to you. I don't have to remind you though that every day without the surgery is another day Rick's heart is stressed."

"I am ready now. The sooner we get started, the sooner it is over."

The observation is tedious. I quickly get bored with the channels on TV, and the walls are starting to feel like they are getting closer. "I am going to lose my mind before this surgery," I half joke to Jacob over the phone.

"I am coming over after class. I have some things for you."

That evening, Jacob and I play chess. I am much better than him. Chess club is one thing I am allowed to do in school, and I have gotten pretty good over the years. As we play, we talk.

"I have not gotten any more emails," Jacob hints. I know what he is talking about, but I really don't want to discuss the low points in my life now. I am so embarrassed about the whole thing.

"I decided email was for old people. I only text now," I joke, trying to lighten the mood. It works.

"I got you a few things today," Jacob says, reaching into his bag.

I wait expectantly. Jacob pulls out a small bracelet that has a small charm on it. I got this at the temple. It's been blessed and will keep you safe during the surgery. I hold the charm up to my face. It is a flat disc with an intricate pattern on it. Underneath the pattern are the words:

Remember, I am always with you.
When you walk
I am behind you, ready to catch you,
Beside you to hold your hand and guide you,
In front of you to lead you,
And when you fall, I will catch you.

I smile softly. The charm is perfect.

"Thanks, Jacob. I'll always have it with me to remind me that I am not alone."

He smiles. "Good. Now how about another game of chess? This time I'm going to beat the pants off you."

The two weeks of observation pass quickly, and before I know it, I am being prepped for surgery. I look at my parents and squeeze my mom's hand. She is crying, and even my dad looks worried. "See you on the other side," I say as everything goes black.

Then I am drifting on an ocean, listening to the sounds of people talking. It makes no sense to me. Slowly I drift out again.

I can hear the people talking again. It sounds familiar. I might know them. I wait to drift out again, but I don't. Instead I feel like I am waking up after a very long night of sleep. I moan, trying to talk to the voices.

"He's awake," they say excitedly.

I open my eyes to see my parents smiling at me. I smile back. "Did I miss anything important?" I ask.

My mom just smiles, and her eyes fill with tears. Suddenly their smiling faces are replaced by Dr Michael's serious face. "How are you feeling?" He pokes and prods me everywhere.

'I am not sure," I say with a smile, "but I am sure you will be able to tell me soon."

"We never have a patient come out of surgery as happy as you are. Usually they are crying," Dr Michael says as he continues to check everything.

I smile again and shrug. "I aim to please."

Finally, he is done, and I appear to be fine. I am glad. I know why those other patients cried. My body feels like it has been run over by a truck. I hurt everywhere and just want to go back to sleep. I drift off.

When I come to again, I am feeling much better. I am still surrounded by my parents. I think my mom must be spending more time here with me than at home. Her usually perfect hair and clothes look terrible.

"Mom, why don't you go home and get some rest? No offence, but you look even worse than I do."

We all laugh, even as my dad starts shooing her out of the room. When she finally leaves, I turn to him and ask.

"Okay, tell me honestly, how did it go?"

"Dr Michael tells me that it went great. The doctors are all very happy with themselves."

I nod, glad to hear the news.

"Great, so when do I get to go home?"

"Well," my dad began, "you have been through a lot, and you need to stay here until you recover."

"Okay…"

"First, you'll spend about a week in the ICU, then you'll be moved over to another ward for rehabilitation."

"How long?"

"About a month."

My jaw drops open. A month! I can hardly comprehend such a long time. Now that I know I am going to be better, I don't want to spend another second being an invalid. I vow to get out of here as soon as possible.

Despite my vow, the hospital keeps me the full month, even though Dr Michael says that I am making great progress. However, time passes much quicker than I thought it would.

Jacob comes by most evenings, but I cannot stay up as late as I used to. He even brings Susan sometimes. Susan is great. Funny and great-looking, just like Jacob deservers.

Soon, the weather starts to warm up, the flowers bloom, and the whole world looks new again. I feel like I am new too. I am going to take control of my life and make sure that I become Rick who happens to have aortic valve stenosis, not an aortic valve stenosis that happens to be named Rick.

There. I've won yet again. I lean back and stretch out my back. It is a gruelling game of solitaire, but I win in the end. Take that, Computer! I look around the room. It is a large office, not like some accounting firms where people are squashed close together. There are about fifteen desks in a big open space. The north wall is solid windows which lets light filter in naturally. My dad thinks this helps people work better as opposed to west windows, which just let the sun in to blind everyone in the afternoon. I think that it just improves the scenery – brown desks, mauve walls, and then a beautiful view of the park five floors below. I swivel my chair and stare out these windows. It looks like a beautiful day. The sky is that wonderful colour of blue that one gets in late summer. There are a few jet trails, but otherwise, nothing breaks the endless expanse of the sky. I close my eyes and pretend I can hear kids playing in the park. What I really hear is the hum of the air conditioner and fifteen computers. It is actually pretty loud in here, I notice. I look around the office. Right now, everyone is busily employed. Well, everyone except me. My dad has once again made sure that I will not be overworked. This means that I finish my work in the morning and then just sit. I used to think it would be fun to get paid to do nothing, but it is not. Instead, doing nothing makes the day drag on forever. I have already played twelve games of solitaire, and it is not even noon.

Crash! Everyone turns to the sound, but we already know what it is. I can't help but smile. I think Ryan drops something at least twice a day. Ryan is my dad's newest employee. He is kind of a misfit here. Everyone else has super tidy desks – I think one of the older guys even sprays his with disinfectant daily. Ryan's desk is the opposite of tidy. He has stacks of paper everywhere. Some are held down with his office supplies, and it is these that fall, disrupting the comparative quiet. This time, it appears to be the stapler dragging a stack of papers with it. I stand up and walk over to help clean up the mess. It doesn't take long to get it cleaned, and I have no excuse to stay and chat, but I do. Before I had surgery, I didn't really talk to anyone in the office. I was too mad at Dad for tricking me into working here so he could keep an eye on me. This time, though, I have a plan, and Ryan is a major part of it. Besides, after talking to him, I have learned that he is a great guy and I sincerely like him, which makes me feel a little guilty about what I am going to do.

"Hey, lost the stapler again?" I tease lightly.

"Well, you know those office supplies, always trying to run away." Ryan laughs. "I should just request for a bigger desk or something."

"It looks like you are falling a little behind this week," I begin.

"Man, it feels like every time I get one task done, there are two more waiting. I am going to have to come in on Saturday again to get it all done. I seem to do so much better when the office is quiet."

I nod. "What about your kids? Don't you guys usually go to the park on the weekends?" We have talked over lunch, and I know Ryan has two little kids at home. He tries to make it to all their soccer games and take them out on the weekends to make up for the fact that their mother passed away a few years ago.

"Yeah, but I really need to get these things done. The kids will understand."

I feel bad for Ryan, I really do. I know he is just on the edge of being let go because of his messy desk and late projects. So I justify to myself what I'm about to do. I'm doing a good deed, helping him look more productive, and therefore, helping him keep his job and spend more time with his kids.

"Tell you what, Ryan. I will just take this little stack for you and get it done this afternoon. That way, you won't have to come in tomorrow."

Ryan looks two parts scared and one part relieved. I don't think people share workloads much here, plus my dad made it abundantly clear about not giving me more work than necessary. Ryan could get into trouble, but I really hope he agrees.

I smile reassuringly. "It will be fine. I already did all mine, and this will help the day go faster for me. If you don't tell my dad, I won't."

Ryan looks confused for a moment. He knows that the reports need to get done, but he knows that he will probably lose his job if my dad finds out.

"Wouldn't it be nice to hang out with the kids this weekend?" I say, trying to sweeten the deal.

He nods. "Knock yourself out. If this works, then maybe your dad won't fire me, and if he does find out, well..." he glances at his desk. "I was probably going to be fired soon anyway." He hands me the stack and winks. "There is more where that came from."

I take the stack back to my desk, trying not to bounce in excitement. I am going to make myself a valuable member of this company.

I finish Ryan's paperwork by the end of the day and drop it off at his desk. "Have a great weekend!" I say with a smile. I know I am going to.

Over the next couple of weeks, I take over more of Ryan's paperwork. I don't feel too bad because I have learned that he is getting what is rightfully my share of the work. We are the new guys, so we get the worst jobs. Or we would have gotten the worst jobs, except this is my dad's company and he has sent out a memo saying I am sick and should not be given extra assignment. Instead, Ryan is getting all the hard jobs, which make him look bad because he cannot get them in on time. It is a vicious cycle, but all that is about to change.

Step 1 of my plan is complete. Now for phase 2.

When I started working here, I used to join my dad for lunch, either in his office or out at nice restaurants. Lunch for him is usually to power meetings with clients. I meet a lot of people we work for, but because my dad is always watching and so careful of me, I have to sit in the background and never get to express my ideas. So I stopped going. Instead, I would pack a peanut-butter-and-jelly sandwich and eat lunch with everyone else. We would laugh and talk for the hour. Soon I know everyone well. I have thought they were just a bunch of fairly stuffy accountants, but they aren't. I also think they thought I was just the spoiled dying son of the boss at first. Now, though, I am changing their minds. It was slow going at first, but now everyone loves me. Luckily for me, getting to know everyone is necessary for the next part of my plan.

I head over to the centre of the room, where Jane, the head of our department, sits. "Hey, Jane," I greet the most important person I need to win completely over. Nothing happens in this office without Jane's approval. Jane has grey hair that is always fashionably arranged, and she wears power suits every day. At first, you think she is this wonderfully powerful older woman, and she is, but Jane is also the office grandmother. She knows everyone's birthday, their kids' names, and always has a special treat to celebrate special days. Just last week, she brought in these bakery mini cupcakes to celebrate the birth of George's son. She got a card that everyone signed and collected money to get George a huge package of diapers. (I guess that is a big deal to a parent; everyone else was super excited about it. I just smile and clap like I knew what the big deal was. I mean, they're diapers. How excited am I supposed to get before it becomes creepy?) If I can win Jane over, then I can finally be a real member of the team.

"How are you today?" Jane says, turning in her chair to look at me better.

"Oh, you know, bored out of my mind." I laugh lightly. "Jane, you know everything that is going on. Give me something to do."

"You know I can't just give you work. What would your father say?"

"He doesn't have to know. You took the Rollins project at the last meeting. How are you going to get all that work done? You're already short-staffed. You know, I would be great at it. Let me help. You can take all the credit. I just want to help."

"Well..."

I can feel her start to give in. I plead, "Please, you know I can do it. I am feeling great. I promise. Don't worry about my dad, he won't find out."

"Rick, you know how your dad feels about this."

"I do, but I also know that you guys are only running behind because I'm not pulling my own weight around here. Honestly, the boredom will kill me a lot faster than a little bit of extra paperwork will."

I give her my most winsome smile and hope against hope. She gives me a considering look and nods as she makes her decision. Jane is always saying that a little work never hurt anyone.

"Fine, but only if you promise me that the moment you start to feel unwell, you quit. I don't want to be responsible for sending you back to the hospital."

She throws me a threatening stare.

"I promise, Jane, I promise." I jump up, excited to get started. Jane's raised eyebrow slows me down. "I really do feel fine, but I won't run in the building," I say with a smile, and Jane smiles and winks at me.

A few more weeks pass, and soon I have taken on enough responsibility to keep me busy all day. I am careful not to overdo it. I remember what it felt like to be too cocky and then have my world come crashing down on me. This time I feel so much better though. I have not even had a hint of pain since the operation. All this while, we are careful to keep this from my dad, better known here as the Boss, as everyone else calls him in respectful fear. The project lists always have someone else's name, and they get the credit, but I do the work. Not the best arrangement, but much better than hundreds of solitaire games.

It is several weeks later, during a family dinner, when the unthinkable happens. I have been lazily eating, my mind still trying to figure out the best way to set up the presentation for a project. I love this work and can't stop thinking about it. I glance out a window and stare at the great view. It is fall again. The oak tree in the backyard is a beautiful mix of shades of red and orange. The colours stand out against the dry green of the spruce near it and the light blue of the sky. At the horizon, the sky is exploding in pinks and purples. *It is good to be alive,* I think. My wandering thoughts are brought quickly back to the present at the mention of Ryan's name.

"I thought I was going to have to fire him at the end of this quarter, but he seems to have gotten things figured out," my dad is saying. It is not uncommon for my parents to discuss the family business at dinner. My mom is well informed about the inner workings of the company.

I smile. My dad still doesn't know that it is me who helps Ryan catch up. Ryan isn't a bad worker; he was just so behind in having to do his work and most of mine that he couldn't do anything well. Once I pitched, he was able to get right back on track fairly quickly. I'm glad that my work saved my friend from losing his job.

"He's not the only one. It seems like Jane's whole department has improved a lot. I'm not complaining, but there is one thing that's been bothering me," he continues. "Many of the employees have been with me for years. I know their personal work style well. Lately though, some of the styles are different. What is even odder is that the changes are all the same. It is like one person is doing parts of all their work."

I almost choke on my food. I've forgotten how smart my dad is. My mom hears the sound and looks over at me. "Honey, are you all right?"

"Yes, Mom," I say, grabbing a glass of water and gulping it down. I duck my head and pretend to concentrate on my spaghetti. I'm going to have to be a lot more careful.

"That is odd. Maybe it is the training course you sent them to last month," my mom reasons.

"Yeah," I speak up, seeing an opportunity to cover my tracks even if it's just a little. "They all said it was a great course.'

"Maybe so, maybe so," my dad reflects.

"So Jacob's got on the honour roll at school," I quickly change the topic.

The conversation turned to Jacob and school. And my dad seemed to forget about the matter, but I was wrong.

On Monday, my dad shows up in the office in the middle of the day just as I am presenting my current project with my team. We are all caught red-handed; it's the same project that George and Ryan are supposed to present to my dad later this afternoon. We all sit in guilty silence, like kids with our hands stuck in the cookie jar, as we wait for the Boss to say something. I am so sure I have gotten my friends in trouble.

"Look, Dad, umm...this isn't as bad as it looks," I began weakly.

"What. Is. Going. On. Somebody explain this to me," he says with anger in his voice.

"I was..."

"You," my dad says, pointing a finger at me. "Be quiet." Then he turns to Jane. "Please tell me what is happening," he says a little calmer.

Jane stands up and tells him everything. How I have been so bored. How I started helping out a little on a few projects but that my work has been good and I have been helping out more and more. She even tells him that now I am assigned projects of my own but that others are listed on the project sheet. "We took it slow, but as you can see, he is really good at it. In the last few months, he has become more valuable to this team than I had thought was possible." She pauses, as if trying to decide whether or not to continue. "And sir, with all due respect, I think you're being too hard on the boy. He has shown more initiative than most people his age. And I have been honoured to work with him. I'm sorry for deceiving you, but I do not regret my decision," she finishes.

Then we all sit in silence.

"Is this true?" my dad speaks so softly we have to strain to hear him. We all nod. He looks around the room then rests his eyes on the screen. "You did this?"

I nod in silence. I have thought of so many things I am going to say to justify my actions, but now that the time is here, I can't think of even one.

"Did you also do the Harrison, Anson, and Smith accounts?"

Again I nod. "I did a lot of those," I acknowledge.

I can see my dad start to soften, even if it is just a little. "Do you know how much your mother and I worry about you? Do you understand that we just want to keep you safe, that *that* is all we have ever wanted for you?"

I nod. Experience has taught me that it is best to acknowledge questions like these silently.

"You are feeling okay? No pains, no weakness, no shortness of breath?"

"I am fine. I have not had any problems for months." It's like it is just the two of us in the room. My dad is staring at me so hard, I think he is trying to see through me. I hold his gaze until he drops his stare and turns back to the projector.

"You really did this work?" he says.

"I did, with some help of course, there is still a lot I am learning."

"You did this?" he repeats himself. I can hear the pride in his voice. I know it is over. Against all reason, my dad is not furious with me. He is proud of me. "That's my son," he says proudly to everyone in the room. They all look relieved at not being in trouble. He grabs me and hugs me, and for some strange reason, everyone starts to clap.

From then on, things have changed. I don't have to do the work behind my dad's back. I get to put my name on the accounts that I help with. I've started to get my own projects. And my dad has started taking me to lunch to talk with clients. And this time, I get to voice my opinions. Some days are good, and some are bad, but I am just the normal guy in the office. And that feels good.

"Flight 1549 to Delhi now boarding," the voice announces in English and then in about five other languages over the airport's intercom system. I look around the airport and grab my luggage – a small laptop. I feel like a real businessman. In fact, I am here in Hong Kong on business. Sometimes it pays to be the son of the boss. It has been a great trip. I love Hong Kong with its tall towers and never-ending flow of traffic. It has been sunny and warm, but now the day appears wet and grey. I am leaving just in time. My only hope is that the rising wind will not make this a bumpy ride. I hate bumpy rides.

I flash my ticket and passport to the agent at the desk and then walk on to the plane. I love flying with this airline. Their first-class section is great. It has a bar and a walking area to stretch your legs. I find my seat, put my stuff in the overhead compartment, and settle in for the ride. Suddenly, I feel a little hand reach through the seat. I turn to see the most angelic-looking baby.

"Hey, how are you?" I coo at her.

"Say *good*," her parents prompt.

"Goo."

"She is so cute."

"Thanks, we hope she is good on this trip." Her parents say with a little smile.

"I am sure she will be perfect. With a face like that, how could she not be?"

Well, I sure am wrong. Apparently, being cute has no impact on a child's behaviour. We have barely lifted off when the little 'angel' shows her true colours. It seems her favourite word is *no*, and she screams it almost constantly at the top of her lungs.

"Noooooooooooooooo!"

The stewardess comes by with my on-board menu, and we try to talk, but I can barely hear her over the screaming baby. Finally, I cannot take it anymore. I get up and leave. I find a different seat in 2G, right next to the bar. As I sit there, I look at all the drinks and people happily drinking away the trip. With the thought *I'll just have one*, I slide up next to the bar.

"Vodka and lime."

One drink relaxes you, two drinks and you feel good, but three drinks and you start babbling to anyone who will listen. So it is no surprise that I find myself telling the barkeeper anything that comes to mind. He is a very understanding person. I guess being barkeeper on a plane lends itself to hearing all sorts of odd stories. I am probably already on my fourth drink when a beautiful girl comes over and whispers in my ear, "Sir, we have your dinner ready."

I take a moment to appreciate her beauty. She has shoulder-length brown hair braided back in a French braid. She has lovely deep brown eyes. I can imagine getting lost in them. She wears her standard uniform but seems to look so much better than the other employees. She has a wonderful smile which she flashes at me again while waiting for my answer.

"Could you give me another fifteen minutes to finish up here?"

"All right, I will come back then."

"Okay," I say, flashing what I hope is a great, flirty smile.

I watch her leave and then turn back to my drink. I intend to go with her in fifteen minutes, but when you are drinking and telling your life story to someone, it can take considerably longer than you think. It seems like only moments have passed when she is right there at my elbow again.

"Are you ready now, sir?"

"Give me another fifteen minutes, please," I say, waving her away, engrossed in the details of my story.

I start into yet another drink and my story when she is back.

"Are you ready for your dinner now?" she says respectfully. She smiles at me, but I can't help noticing that her smile is not so wide, and she seems a little tense.

"Can you give me fifteen more minutes? I just want to finish this drink."

"Okay."

I am just finishing my drink when she is at my elbow again.

"Excuse me, sir."

Her voice is tense like she is speaking through clenched teeth. I turn to look. She is rather upset. In fact, I believe I may just be the person she hates most in the world right now. After all, she probably has to wait until I finish my dinner before she can take a break.

I flash my best smile at her and ask, "Can I have my dinner now?" in the cheekiest voice I can manage. It works. She visibly relaxes, and I know that she no longer wishes to throw me out of the plane.

I follow her back to my seat. The baby has given up and is sleeping peacefully. I sit down, and she gives me a delicious meal. I know everyone makes fun of airline food, and I know why. Usually, it is just one step above school cafeteria food. Today, however, the lunch is wonderful. It is as good as any lunch you would buy in a cafe. I am just finishing up when the pretty girl comes by again. She takes my tray and offers me dessert. I politely accept. I am beginning to feel sorry for how I have been treating her. When I see the dessert, I laugh out loud and do not feel so sorry for her anymore. It appears that she can take care of herself. Dessert is supposed to be a bowl of ice cream, but this looks more like a milkshake, all runny and milky. The chocolate chunks float around like little islands in a sea of milky-white vanilla. I figure I deserve it as I had made her wait, so I eat all of it, right down to the last chunk of chocolate. When she comes back to get the dish, she is surprised to see it all gone. I smile at her, and then she flashes me the best smile I have ever seen before grabbing the plates and heading back to her station.

As time passes and she is off attending to her duties, I try to settle down for the rest of the flight. I try to watch a movie, but it does not hold my attention. I try to read, but my previously exciting book seems dull and dry. I stare out the window, trying to drag my thoughts to anything other than pretty brown eyes and a gorgeous smile. It always surprises me how blue the sky is up here and how the clouds look like you could walk right over them like solid ground. There is nothing else to see out the window though. The clouds cover up even the mountain peaks. My legs are full of energy and bounce unceasingly. This flight seems to be taking forever. Finally, I get up to walk around. I have no destination. I just need to get out some of this energy. I wander all over the plane and am soon in the back, in the galley. The staff have just finished cleaning, and they are standing around, talking. I see her.

"Hey, thanks for a great dinner," I say, trying to start a conversation.

"Just doing my job."

"My name is Rick."

"Lisa."

"Well, Lisa, where are you from?" Just like that, we are talking. We have so much to say to each other. The conversation flows easily. We are both only children. We like to travel and see new things, and we both like the same music. The other flight staff are throwing us inquisitive looks, but I ignore them.

We get to talking about our favourite music.

"There is a great song in the movie *Once Upon a Time in Mumbaai*," I say. "It is...I can't remember the name." I pound my head as if that would shake loose the name of the song. "I know it. Just a minute..."

"Yeah, I've seen that movie. It had a great soundtrack. The song is...Oh, man, I can't remember it either," Lisa says, laughing.

"It is...No, that's not it."

"Must be the altitude," Lisa says. "It makes us forget things all the time. We'll probably remember it as soon as we land."

We start talking about all the other great Bollywood movies we have seen. Surprisingly, we have seen a lot of the same ones.

"Hey, Lisa, it is time to check the cabins again," a co-worker says, tapping her lightly on the arm, and just like that, the conversation is over. I know if I let her go, I will never see her again. So with every ounce of courage, I speak up.

"Lisa, can I email you or add you on Facebook?"

She smiles. "Sure, that would be great. Here is my information." She takes a napkin and writes her information down. I take it. Her handwriting is just as perfect as I thought it would be, but she has only written her name.

"Is there a special picture I should look for to know it is you?" I ask.

"If you remember my face, you will find me," she says as she turns to go back to work.

I smile. There is no way I will ever forget her face. I should have no problem finding her again. I return to my seat, only to find that I am so relaxed after the conversation with Lisa that I fall asleep for the rest of the flight.

"Please prepare for landing," the captain says, waking me up. I look out the window as India comes rushing to greet me. I can see the heat waves shimmering off the road. It is going to be hot again today. I watch the buildings get bigger and bigger until I am the one that feels small again. When the wheels hit the tarmac, I am excited. My family should be waiting for me. My whole family is in Delhi this week for my cousin's wedding. It has been a while since they were all here.

The captain turns off the 'fasten seatbelt' sign, and I grab my laptop. The little baby is waking up, stretching and screwing up her face. I am positive she is going to start crying again. She does. "Maaaaaaa," she whines. I am only too happy to get off the plane. As I leave, I see Lisa.

"It was nice to meet you," I say. "I will get in touch."

Lisa just smiles and continues to help the passengers get off. I continue to walk into the airport. My family is there, running to give me hugs the moment I step out of the door.

I fully intend to keep my promise, but from the moment I step off the plane, I am enveloped by family and wedding plans.

I am putting on my suit to take care of some last-minute business preparations before the weekend and the wedding when I find the napkin again. I run it through my fingers, picturing Lisa. I look in the mirror. I am not a bad-looking guy, but not a great one either. I claim that I am lucky I do not have a whole head of grey with as stressful as my life has been. I wonder if she even remembers me. She sees so many people every day and probably gives out her information every day. Still, I smile. I can hope that I made some sort of impression on her. I lay the napkin gently on my desk and get ready to leave. I will contact her when things have settled down a bit.

The weekend goes fast, and soon I am alone in my room, facing that little square of napkin again. It is taunting me. I pace back and forth in front of it. If she doesn't remember me and I write out of the blue, she will feel like I am stalking her. If she does remember me, I have probably made her mad by waiting for so long to write. I convince myself to just throw the paper away. I am crumpling it up into a little ball to toss into the garbage when I see her smile in my mind. She is so beautiful. I smooth out the ball and spread out the napkin by the keyboard. I sit down, stretch my arms, take a deep breath, and type her full name into the 'Find' bar. The website finds at least twenty Lisas, and I scroll down trying to find her picture. At last, I find it. My memory did not play tricks on me. She is just as beautiful as I remember. I pause for a moment. I can't believe I am about to email a girl I have only spoken to for a few minutes aboard a plane. I try to carefully compose my message in my head, and then I start typing. It takes a few tries, but I finally have it, an email that sounds fun and friendly without being too wordy. I read through again just to be sure.

Hello, Miss Lisa,

Sorry my message came in so late. I was quite occupied with my cousin's wedding.

How are you? I hope your work is keeping you on your toes and taking you to all the exotic places the rest of us only dream about.

Before I forget, the song that we were trying to remember from the movie Once Upon a Time in Mumbaai *was* 'Tum jo aaye'.

Hope you have an incredible day.

Best wishes,

Rick

I hit the 'Send' button and sit back to wait. I don't expect a message right away, but I can't help but stare at my inbox.

The next couple of days went by in an exchange of emails, texts, and instant messages.

Hope I'm not being too nosy, but what exactly do you do when you're not touring the world? So far, all you've talked about has been about work, work, work.

Rick,
6 September, 5.16 p.m.

Lol! Surprisingly, I do spend some time on land, but honestly, whatever time I get, I spend it with my family and friends and work out in gym...when I'm not asleep or being lazy that is!

OK, now it's my turn! What do you do when you are out of your busy schedule?

Lisa,
6 September, 6.03 p.m.

Haha! As you can see, it took me a while to answer that one. You can either say I'm always busy or that I don't really have much to do outside work. I have a big family, so they are really my social life.

Rick,
6 September, 6.45 p.m.

Well then I'd say you need to get out more. What about all the 616 friends you have on your Facebook page?

Lisa,
6 September, 7 p.m.

600 of them that don't care I exist? I write poetry though. Once in a while I do my part for charity, and I guess I like to hike as well when I remember I need the exercise. But to be honest, I really don't do much.

Rick,
6 September, 7:15 p.m.

Wow, poetry? Now that's very interesting! What kind of poetry do you write? I remember a friend in school wrote poetry, and I can appreciate the talent, and writing poetry is very worthwhile...

Lisa,
6 September, 7.30 p.m.

This was how our friendship grew.

As the days turned into nights and the nights became weeks, I found myself in the middle of sending Lisa a message at least twelve times a day, and with the speed and frequency of her replies, I'm sure she was equally preoccupied.

For some reason, it didn't occur to either of us to pick up the phone and call. No doubt it would definitely have made things easier, but I think we were caught up in the adventure/fantasy/ excitement of it. Maybe it was the thrill of anticipating a reply, or was it that we were having too much fun? Or maybe we just didn't want to jinx it.

Whatever it was, Lisa and I kept in touch constantly.

I think I can safely call you an owl. You don't seem to know the meaning of sleep. Do you know this is the third night in a row that you've been up past twelve?

> Rick,
> 13 September, 2.15 a.m.

Hahaha! It's because I do a lot of night flights. My body just got used to it, I guess. Is this your way of telling me you're tired and sleepy? :p Old man can't stay awake past 8 p.m.

> Lisa,
> 13 September, 2.30 a.m.

Oh! Makes sense now. Tired? Me?!! Never! But just to be clear, if for some reason my next couple of messages looks like Hindu French...I'm not sleep-typing...that was my plan all along.

> Rick,
> 13 September, 2.35 a.m.

ROTFL! Hahahah! Goodnight, Rick, get some sleep so I can torment you again tomorrow night.

> Lisa,
> 13 September, 2.40 a.m.

"What's wrong with your face?" my brother asked one day when he strolled into my room as I furiously typed out a witty reply to one of Lisa's comments.

"My face? Nothing's wrong with my face. What do you mean?"

"It's like your ears are in a tug of war for your mouth! You've been smiling all day!"

"I'm smiling because I hear that's what happy people do," I replied light-heartedly, throwing a nearby sock at him.

'Rick Puri? Happy people? Now that is something." He laughed back, dodging the missile. I could hear him seconds later in the corridor, telling anyone who listened how I had just confessed to being happy, like it was breaking news from the Taj Mahal. But how could I deny it?

I was still smiling.

◎

I just downloaded that song from that movie we were talking about. 'Jhalak Dikhlaja' by Himesh Reshammiya. Wish I had written this. :(

Rick,
18 September, 10.45 a.m.

You really like music, don't you?
Am I going to get a chance to read one of your poems?

Lisa,
18 September, 11 a.m.

I do actually. How about I write one especially for you?

Rick,
18 September, 12 p.m.

*Really?! I'd like that, but I don't mind your old ones too,
you know. I'd love to read them.*

Lisa,
18 September, 12.20 p.m.

I hesitated to show Lisa my poetry – brooding, melancholic verses often centred on me. You would not be wrong if you said I was worried about what she might think. Everything was going so well, and I was afraid that if she knew who I once was, things might change.

Sitting outside a cafe, with a cup of just what the doctor ordered steaming in front of me, tasteless green tea to you and me, I leaned back to soak in the fresh air. I had given myself plenty of time to wait for my next client by getting there early, so I passed the time by sending Lisa another message on my phone. By this time, we were in steady communication. There was nothing odd about receiving a text or an email at 1 a.m., which led me to think about where exactly our relationship was going.

Tentatively, I had begun calling what we had a relationship, but was it really? It seemed like a minute didn't go by without a thought of Lisa passing through my mind. Barely a month into meeting this woman, I already felt a deeper connection with her than I have ever felt with friends I have known for years.

Deep in thought about how and if I should take our relationship to the next level, it occurred to me that she might not feel the same way. (Maybe she was just humouring a sick man?) Then suddenly it hit me; she didn't know. In all our discussions, from early morning till late at night, some of them long sessions in which I had poured my heart and soul out, I had somehow neglected to tell her this most important fact. It also dawned on me that this was the real reason why I was reluctant to show my poetry; it was a window to my past that I had so far pretended did not exist.

A familiar beep of an incoming message woke me from my thoughts. Picking up my phone, I saw what I already knew. It was a message from Lisa; my heart skipped a beat for the third time that afternoon, but this time, it was for a completely different reason.

You know you can call me if you feel like you need to talk to someone. You still have my card, right?

Rick,
25 September, 6.14 p.m.

Yes, I still have it. Why do you think I want to talk to somebody?

Lisa,
25 September, 6.20 p.m.

I don't know. I just had this feeling that you were not happy about something (sad even?) and maybe you needed somebody to listen. I have a degree in mind-reading, you know? (Plus you mentioned it an hour ago.)

Rick,
25 September, 6.25 p.m.

Okay.

Lisa,
26 September, 9 p.m.

I waited, and I waited.

While my heart raced with a mix of emotions, my head plagued me with a million questions. Would she call? What if she didn't? What if she did? What would I say? What would she say? Maybe she was annoyed with me for presuming so much? What if she decided she never wanted to speak to me again? I was on a mental roller coaster.

I woke up the next day, fearfully scrambling for my phone. Sure I had fallen asleep and missed her call, but there was no missed call and there was no message. For risk of looking like a selection of things – stalker, desperate, jerk to name a few – I decided not to send Lisa a message that morning; instead, I waited for her to make the first move. Needless to say, I checked my phone every thirty minutes that day, but there was no email, no text, no chat message. It was as if she had dropped off the face of the communication world. By the end of the day, I had given up on hearing from her and begun to ask myself if I should take the bull by the horns and be the one to reach out first. After all, I was the one who rocked the boat; I had to be the one to save us from drowning.

I had finally decided on a course of action, to blow the whole thing off, like it had never happened. Maybe she'd lost her phone? Maybe her Internet was down? There could be a countless number of perfectly innocent reasons behind the silence, and I was just panicking for nothing. And then my phone rang.

It was a number I had never seen before, but somehow I knew it was her.

"Hello, tortoise," she said. The familiar use of the nickname sent my pulse racing to new speeds.

"Hello, rabbit," I replied, as coolly as I could manage.

"Do you know who is speaking? Or do you call every strange woman you meet on a plane rabbit?"

"Of course I know who this is, and don't forget, you came up with the names yourself, Lisa."

"Okay, you got me there," she replied, laughing. Her laugh, like a beautiful musical instrument, seemed to cover the hundreds of miles between us so that it felt like she was practically next door.

"Hmm, interesting," I said, "you sound nothing like I imagined."

"Is that so? What did you imagine, and how do I sound?" she asked, and I could almost picture the smile on her face.

"Oh, I don't know. I thought you might sound like nails on a blackboard, but you're lucky it's just a chainsaw."

"Ha ha ha! I should be offended."

"But you're not, because it's not true. You have a beautiful voice and the most musical laugh I have ever heard."

"Aww, thank you!" she replied shyly. "Now you're just making me blush."

"That's the plan. So what took you so long? I thought I would never hear from you again."

"Really? Ha ha! That's really sweet."

"Not for me. I spent the whole day worrying that I had offended you somehow."

"I'm sorry. I was just trying to decide if it was the right thing to do, but I'm here now, and that's all that matters, right?"

It is.

Weeks later, at the end of a meeting, while everyone was filing out of the boardroom, I had what I thought was a brilliant idea, so I stayed behind in my seat to make a phone call.

"Hey, Lisa. You know I'm in Delhi, right?"

"Yes, I know. You told me."

"Would you care to have lunch with me?"

"What? Face to face?"

"Yes, Lisa. That's usually how it works," I replied with a laugh.

"Uhh…I don't know," she replied thoughtfully. "I don't know if it's a good idea."

"Why not? I know you haven't had lunch yet, and even if you have had, I know you can still eat more." I paused for the rewarding sound of her laughing. "Plus, for some reason, I'm beginning to think I'm talking to Nokia's customer care! I've almost forgotten what you look like. Or do I have to get on a plane to see you again?"

I could practically hear her weighing the pros and cons in her head. I was past mental doubt at this point and had stopped second-guessing myself and what role I played in her life. Since we began talking on the phone – a development we both agreed should have happened sooner – I had made it clear where I stood and how I felt about her, and I took her continued communication with me as a good sign.

"You don't want me to have a bad experience in your own city, under your very nose, do you?" I continued. "And you can finally show me that place you claim makes great cold coffee."

"I see why you're so good at your job," she replied with a sigh of defeat. "Fine, I'll meet you at the Lifestyle Mall in an hour. Ask a taxi to take you there. Everybody knows where it is."

"Great! See you in an hour."

She walked towards me, beautiful, graceful, and confident.

"Well, well, well, Mr Rick Puri," she said, taking a seat opposite me with a huge smile on her face. "Finally, we meet again."

"Would have happened sooner or later, right? With or without a plane ticket."

She laughed loudly, throwing her head back, which made me smile at how at ease she was with me. "You know, you almost missed me. Remember that flight I'm supposed to be on the day after tomorrow?" she asked, and I nodded in recollection as I signalled for the waiter. "Well, it's been moved to tomorrow instead," she concluded quietly. I could see her bracing herself for my reaction, and I admit I did nothing to disguise my unhappiness. Even the waiter muttered something about having to get a new pen and hurried away.

"But tomorrow is just the day after today!" I cried bitterly.

"I know, I'm so sorry!" she replied apologetically. "One of the crew members had a family emergency, so I was called in. I'm really sorry, and I will try and make it up to you. Maybe tomorrow we can go to the temple, and I'll take you to all those places I'm always telling you about?" She reached out to take my hand with a very apologetic smile. I mumbled a very grumpy consent, causing her to laugh even more at my whining, but I held her hand anyway.

The thing about imagination is, that compared to the reality, it is never quite what you thought it would be, one way or another. This day was just like that. I had imagined seeing Lisa again, what that day would be like, and all the things we would do and talk about. The reality was nothing compared to that. I could not have imagined her laughter or how bright and clear and cool the weather would be, and how her hair shone in the sun. And when night came, the stars were not to be outdone either. Quite simply said, it was a picture-perfect day.

The next day, Lisa and I made arrangements to meet at one of the city's most famous temples. Approaching the temple's entrance, I was in a dark-blue kurta, and Lisa was in a white-and-gold sari, over which I accused her of wanting to blend in with the angels. All I felt was pride as we walked in together. The rest of the day breezed by, so I guess it's true about time flying when you're having fun. It wasn't very long before Lisa had to change and leave for the airport, but I think if I had been given a week, I would still think the time was too short. I offered to take her to the airport, my attempt to prolong the inevitable, but all that did was make driving back alone in the car seem quiet without her cheerful voice and contagious laughter.

With nothing but my thoughts for company, I remembered the last time I had been in Amritsar. It wasn't too long ago, and even then, I had visited the temple, but I had gone there alone. Then I had prayed for guidance and strength, and to find the person that God had made for me. Walking into that temple today with Lisa by my side, I knew my prayers had been answered.

That night, I dream of Amy. Well, not really *of* Amy. I dream about the day I told her about me and how sick I was. She was completely blindsided by the information. To be fair, I think she would have responded the same way, no matter how she found out. I realize on my way home after dropping off Lisa that I would have to tell her someday, and I am scared. I am absolutely terrified of losing her. It is this realization that leads to the dream with Amy. I wake up covered in sweat. I can no longer sleep, so I get up and take a shower. Then I sit at the computer and stare at the screen. I make a half-hearted attempt to watch a movie, but nothing works to distract me from my thoughts. Finally, I fall back to sleep, absolutely exhausted. This time I don't dream of anything.

I spend the next few days trying to decide what to do. For a few hours, I consider not telling her. Then I think of how Amy found out about my condition and at the same time how she found out that I might die, and I decide I don't want to make the same mistake my seventeen-year-old self did. I want to do it right this time. But how do you even bring up the topic? "Speaking of lipids, I have a lot of extra lipids in my blood?" What about saying, "Speaking of scars, would you like to see the scars from my heart surgery?"

This is why I am stuck. In my whole life, I have never actually been the person that broke the news to someone else. It was always my parents, teachers, or doctors who told everyone. It is just not something that comes up in normal conversation. I can only think of one way to do it. In person. That way, I can see her reaction and know how much to tell her.

I am at work, pacing around my office, when the phone rings. I have set it up so that when Lisa calls, it plays *'Tum jo aaye'* from *Once Upon a Time in Mumbaai*. The caller ID says *Rabbit*.

"Rabbit!"

"Hi, tortoise."

"Guess who was on the plane this afternoon?"

"Umm?"

"Jackie Chan."

"Na-uh! Did you talk to him?"

"I did. I asked him if he was ready for his dinner. He said I should give him fifteen more minutes."

I laugh. "I am sure he was just trying to get your attention."

"He was busy reading a script and did not want to get food on it." She laughs. "He was much nicer than some other people I know."

"Oh yeah, that is much more practical than wanting to drink some more vodka."

I could almost see her smile. "What are you doing?"

"Just working, trying to figure out the best way to present this information to a new customer."

"I'll let you go then."

"No, no. I am at a good stopping point."

"So I had a lot of fun the other day. Do you want to go out again soon?"

I am so shocked. She truly is the rabbit now. "I would love to. This weekend?"

"Sure."

I am about to add more when there is a knock on the office door, and I have to go. I hang up and reluctantly return to business.

On Friday, I make my decision. I am going to tell her this weekend. First, though, we are going to have the perfect day: picnic in the park, a visit to the museum, and a fancy dinner. When I talk to Lisa again, I will tell her I have a surprise planned for the weekend and will take care of all the arrangements. I add, "If that's okay with you." She assures me that she can't wait to see what I have planned.

I go to the store and pick up the traditional picnic basket and tablecloth. While a picnic can be an impromptu affair with peanut butter and jelly sandwiches eaten on an old blanket, I want this picnic to be like the picnics from the movies. Someday I will have to look back on this day, and I want the memories to be warm and fuzzy, not cold and bleak.

I go to the deli on Saturday and pick out the best sandwiches they have. I add a bottle of wine and some fruit that I know Lisa likes. I have real plates and wine glasses for us to use. I pack them all carefully in my basket before I go to pick up Lisa. I call the restaurant and confirm our reservation for tonight. I request a nice, quiet window table if it is available. Then I get dressed in nice slacks and a polo shirt and head out the door. As I close the door, it occurs to me that when I open it again, I will either be on top of the world or at the bottom.

Lisa looks beautiful as always. Today she has chosen to wear slacks with platform sandals. The effect makes her legs look super long and trim. Her blouse is light blue and casual. Her hair is pulled back in the braid I love, and long dangly earrings swing by her cheeks. I sit stunned for a moment. She sees me and runs up to the car, jumping in the passenger's side.

"So what's on the docket for today, tortoise?"

"We are going to start with a picnic," I say, swinging the car out into traffic.

The day goes well, much better than I could have planned for. We take off our shoes and walk though the grass; we watch the kids playing in the lake and laugh at their antics. When I tell Lisa that our next stop is a museum, she is silent. I have learned to take this particular silence as an unwillingness to hurt my feelings by disagreeing with me. When I tell her the name of the museum, she is excited. It is a Bollywood museum that recently opened that she hasn't had a chance to visit because of her job.

At the museum, we are both fascinated by the same exhibit, a display of things belonging to our favourite Bollywood actor. We laugh at some of the things he acquired through his movies and travels. They seem so fitting, considering his movies. We are at the museum for hours, and we still don't see everything, but we are soon tired and hungry.

"Come on, I have a wonderful dinner planned," I say as we step out into the cold night air. It is still early spring, and while the days may be warming up, the nights are cold. I wrap my arm around Lisa's shoulder to keep her warm, and we get back to my car. Lisa is silent. I turn on the heater to warm us up, and we drive to the restaurant to the sound of the radio. I am worried that I have ruined things by wrapping my arm around her. I am about to apologize when she slips her hand into mine. For a moment, I know it is all going to be okay. Then I remember what I am planning on doing tonight, and I get worried again.

When we get to the restaurant, the valet opens Lisa's door and helps her out before coming around to my door to get the keys. I look at Lisa from over the top of the car. She flashes me her best smile, the one that says 'I like you'. We walk into the restaurant, holding hands, and my heart skips a few beats. This must be what it feels like to have everything.

◎

It takes a few minutes for our eyes to adjust to the dim interior of the restaurant. It smells like spices, cooking bread, and a little like fresh earth. Far overhead, small lights twinkle like little stars. There are small table lamps on each table, so each table is a little island of romantic lights. Unlike most restaurants where you are crowded into a booth or sitting at a small table in the middle of the floor with a hundred people surrounding you, this restaurant has each table in its own little alcove. We follow the waiter to our table, passing through a maze of fountains, bushes, flowers, and small French dividers. We walk on a bridge with a small stream flowing under it. Lisa leans over and whispers in my ear, "I have never been somewhere so fancy. Thank you." Finally, we arrive at our table. We sit down and are immediately out of touch with the world. It is like only we exist here in our own little Eden.

We order some wine and appetizers right away and then peruse the menu. Everything looks delicious. In fact, everything is delicious. The dinner is great, the company is wonderful, but I can't stop thinking about what I plan on telling Lisa tonight. It ruins some of the mood for me. We finish, pay our bill, and are escorted back to the entrance. I am glad because I don't know if I could have found my way back through the maze.

"What's the matter? You seem kind of tense."

"Well, I need to talk to you about something, and I am not really sure how you will take it," I say.

"You have a wife?" Lisa says, joking.

I smile. "As a matter of fact...," I pause dramatically. "No, I do not."

"What is it? Only the girls are supposed to get all tense about the talk." She makes little hand quotes around the words *the talk*.

"No, it is not that. Although afterwards, maybe we should have that talk."

We are now at Lisa's house. I park the car, turn off the engine, and turn to face her. "Lisa, I have to tell you something. I think you have a right to know." I pause for a minute, not really sure how to begin. She waits patiently, but her smile fades a little.

"You are scaring me, Rick. What is the matter?"

"Okay, I have aortic valve stenosis?"

"Aortic what?"

"Aortic valve stenosis. You know how your heart has four chambers and valves to keep the blood in those chambers? Well, my aortic valve, the one that keeps blood from dropping back down into the heart after it is pumped into the body, is too small." I pause and watch her face. She seems to be taking it all in. "This means that at first, when I was little, my heart had to pump extra hard to get blood out to my body. It puts a lot of stress on the heart."

"Now that you are not little anymore?"

"As a teenager, I had two surgeries to fix the problem. They were very risky surgeries. The second one had a higher chance of killing me than saving me."

"So, are you cured?"

"Yes. Right now, the only difference between me and anyone else is the scar on my chest."

She smiles at me.

"How did you get it? Were you born with it, or was it something that you developed later?"

"I got it as I got older. I was born with something else, something called hyperlipidaemia."

"And what is that exactly?"

"Well, I have too much fat in my blood. It helped cause the heart problem by depositing fat on my arteries and essentially causing the narrowing of the aortic valve."

"But you are okay now, right? You are not telling me this because you have another risky surgery next week, are you?" Lisa looks at me with concern.

"No, I am okay. I just wanted you to know before things got more serious between us. I thought you had a right to know. Some girls don't want to be with a defective person."

"I care about you. It doesn't matter to me if your heart is not perfect. I would not care if you were missing a leg. I love you for who you are. If you are willing to keep dating me, I am willing to do anything and experience anything with you."

"Lisa, there may be problems in the future. I am proud of my grey hair because they mean that I have beaten the odds so far. I might not be so lucky the next time."

"We can get through anything together," she says, melting my heart.

"Thank you," I say and lean against my seat.

"I guess we had 'the talk' after all," Lisa jokes, lightening the mood.

I smile and go around helping her out of the car. As I walk her to her door, I cannot believe how lucky I am to have this woman in my life. God is surely blessing my life. At her door, I turn to her. She looks up at me with her big brown eyes. I bend down and gently kiss her lips. I let my fingers touch her check and run thought her hair. I kiss her once more. She smiles at me. "I love you."

"I love you too," she answers. The sound of her saying it fills me with warmth. We sit on her doorstep and talk till it is too cold for it to be comfortable. Reluctantly, I let her go inside. As I walk back to my car, I feel like I am floating down the steps.

Lisa and I spend all our free time together now. We talk at least once a day, but we usually lose count. She will call while she is on the bus going to work, or I will call while I am driving home. We try to get together on our days off when we both have the same schedule. We are getting very serious and have even talked about getting married. It is a big step. About two weeks ago, I was able to talk Lisa into meeting with my doctor so she will know exactly what she is getting if she decides to marry me. I set up a special appointment. First, there was a physical test to make sure that I am in great health now. Then we sat down and talked about my condition. Lisa spent a lot of time asking questions about my health. She has thought about it a lot more than I have realized. All the doctors assure us that I am healthy. They all like Lisa and ask to be invited to the wedding. I am nervous that we are even thinking about getting married. All that is left was to meet each other's parents and get permission.

Last week, we went out to dinner with my parents. It was just a casual one at a restaurant. Lisa was terrified to meet my parents despite my reassurances that they would love her. She dressed carefully, and in my car, on the way to meet them, she chewed her nails. I grabbed her hand and once again told her that my parents would love her. The dinner went amazingly well. Even better than I thought it would. My parents love her. I think they would like almost any girl who would be willing to stay with me after hearing about my problems. However, they like Lisa for more than that. She had my dad, a stuffy businessman, laughing out loud at her tales of working with people. My mom was thrilled with her love of travelling and adventure. My mom had once been a traveller too. She had so many questions for Lisa about how exotic cities have changed since she was last there. As I said, the dinner was great. My parents even told me that night that I should do whatever it takes to keep Lisa.

Now, though, it was my turn to be nervous. Lisa was going to set up a time for me to meet her parents. I hope I can impress them. I can give presentations to lots of people for work without getting nervous, but meeting her parents scares me. Now I know why she was biting her nails. As I pace and worry, the phone rings. It is Lisa.

"I am so mad at him," she snarls as soon as I greet her.

"Him, who?"

"My dad! I told them about you and how we wanted to take them out for lunch. They were all excited for me and started asking questions. I told them all about you. How you are sweet and charming. How smart you are. One thing led to another, and I told them about your heart problem. All of a sudden, the mood changed. My dad was no longer smiling and nodding. He says that I should not see you again. That you are no good for me. He thinks that you will hold me back and make it so I can't do all the things I want. I tried to make him see that all I want is you, but he just won't."

"Well," I say, trying to be understanding, "that is not the best start, but maybe with time he will change his mind."

I can almost feel her relax through the phone. "Maybe, but you don't know my father. He rarely changes his mind. I guess it is not all bad news. My mom agreed to have lunch with us on Wednesday. She says she will wait until she knows you before telling me that you are no good. She will love you, though."

Now I am really nervous. I am going into this with Lisa's parents already not liking me. I hope I can make a good impression.

On Wednesday, I take an extra-long shower and put on two squirts of deodorant. The place where we are meeting is pretty casual. I have to work so I can't be dressed too casual, but I don't want to be too formal either. I decide to go with my favourite pair of khaki slacks and a green polo.

I meet Lisa and her mom at a bistro we have found weeks earlier while window shopping. It has become one of our favourite places to come to. I love this place. There are old records and movie posters stapled to the wall. The records are always the same, but the movie posters change with time. I always spend a few minutes looking at the new ones to see if I have seen the movies being advertised. The tables are a garish red with metal legs, and the chairs are simple wicker stools. There is always some sort of weird international music playing over the speakers, just loud enough to be heard but not so loud that you have to yell over it. Despite the terrible taste in decorating, the food is excellent. Even if all you order is a coffee, it comes with little biscotti that taste out of this world. I see Lisa and her mom as soon as I walk in. Lisa's mom looks like a slightly older and rounder version of Lisa. She is probably in her early fifties, but looks like a forty-year-old. Her hair is cut short and permed in the popular fashion. They are both drinking tea and talking animatedly. Lisa and her mom have spent the day shopping together and have the bags to prove it. From what little Lisa has told me about her family, I have come to understand that Lisa has always been pretty close to her mom.

"Hi, ladies," I say, walking towards them. I shake hands with Lisa's mom. "I am Rick, and you must be Mrs Johnson."

"Nice to meet you."

I sit down beside Lisa and squeeze her knee reassuringly. I am not sure if it is to reassure myself or her that things will go well. "What have you guys been buying today?" I say with a smile.

"Well, we got some new pictures for my mom's living room. They are just perfect. It was like they were painted for her house. Show him, Mom," Lisa says excitedly. I look at the pictures, and they are nice, but I am too nervous to fully appreciate them. I am trying to decide what to say next when the waiter comes and takes our order. I am relieved for the interruption. As he is leaving, a popular song comes on. We start taking about it, and the conversation begins to flow. Soon we are chatting like old friends about movies, songs, people we would like to meet, and how great the food here is. I start to feel comfortable and even make some jokes that Lisa's mom laughs at. Then we are done eating, and the conversation turns serious.

"There is no polite way to ask this, so I will just come right out and ask," Lisa's mom says. I wait. I have known this was coming. "Just how sick are you?"

"Not at all. I can do everything that everyone else can do. In truth, I am completely healthy."

"Are you sure? I have heard stories about men marrying and then getting super sick so their wife grows old before their time taking care of them."

"I would never do that to Lisa. Not on purpose anyway. I obviously don't know what the future holds any more than you do. All I can do is reassure you that I am completely healthy today and odds are good that it will continue that way."

I can see that she is still hesitant. I have not dispelled any of her fears. I am prepared for this. "If you would like, I can show you my medical records, and you can go over them to make sure I am not lying to you."

"No, I believe you. I am just nervous. What if something bad happens?'

At this point, Lisa speaks up. She reaches across the table and holds her mom's hand in hers. "Mom, no matter who I marry, something bad could happen. We have all heard the freak stories about grooms getting run over as they come out from the wedding. I have been to the doctors with Rick, and I have talked with them. They are super friendly and kind. They answered all my questions and told me that Rick is as healthy as anyone else. I told them that my parents might be nervous, and they said that you were welcome to call as long as they get to attend the wedding."

I smile. They have joked about being able to come to the wedding and even asked for the date.

"I just don't know," Lisa's mom says hesitantly.

"Mrs Johnson, I assure you that I am healthy. I love your daughter and will do anything you ask of me to be allowed to marry her. I will wait forever for her if that is what it requires to make you comfortable with it." I stop and think about what I just said. "But please don't make me wait that long."

She smiles at me. "I like you, Rick. I really do. You are funny and just as charming as my daughter said you would be. I know that you love her and that she loves you. Maybe someday you will understand my fear. She is my only daughter. When she marries, she will leave me forever."

"No, I won't."

"You will. It is the nature of life. I just want to know that you will be happy, that I am not letting you rush into something that will make you miserable in a few years. I only want the best for you."

"Rick is the best for me, Mom. I know he is."

"I know, honey, I know," Lisa's mom concludes, shaking her head in concentration. She looks at her watch. "I have to be going.

I have an appointment in a few minutes." She grabs her bags and gets ready to leave, then she leans over the table towards me. She is very serious. "I will speak to my husband. I will tell him the things you have told me. He may want to talk to your doctors before he believes you. However, if he met you, I think he would like you. He can be very stubborn though. Once he decides something, it is very hard to change his mind. I will do my best." Then she turns to Lisa. "I love you, and I am happy for you. I will talk to your father and try to help you." With that, she leaves.

Lisa and I sit quietly for a while. Lunch hour is over, and we are the only ones left. We can hear the music and the sounds of the kitchen being cleaned in the back. The air smells like ten different meals all mixed together. It is actually a very good smell. I take a deep breath. "I think that went well."

"My mom really likes you. I could tell. She had her happy smile. If she didn't like you, she would have smiled more like this." Lisa shows me what the smile would have looked like. I laugh.

"That is the smile you gave me when we first met!"

"Yeah, we are pretty similar that way."

We talk for a while, enjoying the solitude. Then she has to go, and so do I. I get her a cab and kiss her as I help her inside. "I will talk to you tonight," I say as she shuts the car door.

The rest of the day passes in a blur. I work. I am lucky to have a job that takes my mind off things when I focus on it. Today, I really focus on my tasks to avoid focusing on Lisa's parents. Then work is over, and I have to go home to face my own thoughts. I find that I am offering up a little prayer almost continually. "Please help Mr Johnson change his mind about me. Please help him like me." I eat dinner and watch a little television. I am not really expecting Lisa to call tonight because she has to work, but when the phone rings, I pick it up, hoping it is her. It is not her though. I look at the caller ID; it is Mrs Johnson.

"Hello, this is Rick."

"Hi, Rick. This is Lisa's mom."

"Hi, how are you doing?" It is not the most stimulating conversation, but I am nervous.

"I just wanted to tell you that my husband has agreed to meet you. Would you like to come over for dinner on Sunday?"

"I would love to. What time?"

"How about eight?"

"Sounds great. Thank you."

"No problem, bye."

"Bye," I say and hang up the phone. I sit back on the couch and stare into space. I am already nervous about Sunday. This is going to be a long week.

I feel like a girl. I have tried on so many clothes, getting ready for tonight. I want to be sure that I look perfect because people really do judge on appearances and I need to make a great first impression on Lisa's father tonight. I finally settle on tan slacks, a light-blue shirt and a blazer. I grab the bottle of wine and flowers I have bought as a gift and leave to pick up Lisa. I am a little early, but I would rather die than be late today.

Lisa's parents live in a large older home. It is surrounded by large trees and a lush lawn. I admire the flower bed as we climb the stairs. It looks like Mrs Johnson is a careful gardener. There is not a single out-of-place stem in the whole bed. Lisa looks at me and squeezes my free hand as she opens the door. "Mom, we are here," she calls. A large dog comes bounding towards us. Lisa bends down and rubs him behind his ears as he licks her face. I stand in the entryway awkwardly. When she is done greeting her dog, she leads me to the kitchen, where her mom is putting the finishing touches to the dinner. I can see her dad through the glass doors, setting up a table. I swallow nervously as Mrs Johnson turns to me. "Hi, Rick," she says nicely.

"Here," I say, holding out the flowers and wine, "I brought a little something for you."

"Oh, thanks. I will just go put these in some water. Make yourself at home." With that, she turns away, busy again. Now is the part I have been dreading all week; it is time to meet Lisa's father.

Lisa takes my hand and leads me to the door. Standing on tiptoe, she whispers in my ear, "It will be okay." Then she gives me a quick kiss and opens the door.

"Daddy, we are here." She gives him a big hug. It is easy to see that they are very close as he hugs her back. He is tall, almost six feet, and has to stoop a bit to hug her. His hair is greying, and he has a little bald spot on the top. He looks like he is in great shape; he doesn't have even the slightest hint of a belly. He is dressed in jeans and a T-shirt, and I hope I am not overdressed. He looks over Lisa, and I can see him studying me. "Daddy, I want you to meet Rick," Lisa says as she comes over and wraps her arm around me. "Rick, Daddy."

"How are you, sir?" We make small talk for a while, but even with Lisa helping us out, the conversation is strained and moves in short jerks and spurts. If the conversation were a car, it would be one of those that is so beat up, you have to push start and then dive in, hoping it won't stop. I think we all breathe a sigh of relief when Lisa's mom brings out the wine and announces that dinner is ready.

"It is such a nice evening, I thought we could eat outside," she says, pointing to the picnic table. We all take our places. The dinner looks wonderful, and I tell Lisa's mom so. She thanks me, and then there is silence. Not that comfortable silence where you are all friends, but that awkward silence when you are waiting for something big to happen. Lisa and her mom chat, trying to draw us in. I answer their questions about work and my week, but we just all seem to be trying to ignore the elephant in the room – Lisa's dad. We are done eating, and Lisa's mom has gone in to get dessert when her dad finally starts talking.

"Look, you seem like a nice-enough guy, but I don't want you with my daughter," he says, pointing his whole arm in my direction. He is still holding his wine glass, and it gives him an imperial air.

"Daddy!" Lisa stares at her father in shock.

"Sir, I understand how you feel, but you should know that I love your daughter very much. I would never do anything to hurt her."

"No, you don't understand. I agreed to this dinner because my wife begged me, but I have no intention of letting my only daughter marry someone who is sick."

"Yes, sir. However, I am not sick. My doctors and medical records will show you that I have been in great health for several years now. I haven't even had a cold in years."

"I don't care what your doctors say."

"That isn't fair." Lisa stands up. I have never seen this side of her. It looks like she is just as stubborn as her father.

"I am your father, and I say I do not want you seeing this boy anymore," her father says, this time pointing at me with his finger. He has also stood up. For a moment, I worry that this may get ugly, but their voices haven't even been raised. They are still talking in their normal voices, just a little more tensely than usual. "He is sick and will not be able to give you the things you deserve."

"He is not sick. I have talked to his doctors, and he is fine. I love him. Even if he were completely debilitated and stuck in the hospital, I would still love him."

Lisa's mother has returned with dessert. She stops mid-stride when she sees what is going on. Together the two of us stand silently and listen.

"He has had surgeries. His heart is still bad. He cannot run. He cannot play sports. He could *die*. He is not good enough for you."

"You are wrong. He is perfect for me. What if I had a brother and he had a few surgeries when he was little? Would you never let him marry because he might one day die and leave his family? We all die eventually. It is how we live that matters. Would you have me live miserably?"

"You know that is not what I want. You are still young. You will find someone else, someone who is healthy."

Lisa looks like she is on the verge of tears. I have been standing (it is weird sitting when everyone else is standing), and I walk over and put my arm around her.

"Sir, I do not want to be a source of contention. It was never my intention to cause a fight between you and your daughter. It is easy to see that you both love each other very much. However, I also love her, and I am willing to fight for her."

He just stares at me. I can feel how much he dislikes me. "Get out of here!"

I move my feet further apart, planting them firmly. I have no intention of leaving. Lisa notices my determination and comes to my side.

"Rick, maybe it would be better if you left. I will call you tonight after we have sorted this out," she says, gently tugging on my arm. I don't want to go, but I can see in her eyes that this is hard on her and she really believes it would be better if I were not there. She takes my arm and tugs it gently. I let her lead me through the house and to the front door. "I love you, and I will get my father to see reason," she says, giving me a goodbye kiss.

I drive home in a daze. *How can that have gone so bad?* I wonder. I knew he did not like me, but he had not even given me a chance. All because of this little defect I have in my heart. I stomp into my living room and flop on the couch despondently. I turn on the TV out of habit, but I don't really watch it. Instead, I wonder what is happening as Lisa and her parents decide my future happiness.

Several hours pass before Lisa calls me. She is sobbing into the phone, and I can hardly make out her words. When I finally understand that her father has forbidden her to see me again, I am furious. I want to yell or throw my phone, but the crying on the other end brings me to my senses. "It's okay. It's okay," I console her.

"I don't know what to do," Lisa moans. "I don't want to lose you, but I can't just ignore my father. He is my dad, and I love him too. Why does it have to be so hard?"

"Shhh...We don't need to figure everything out right now. Everything is going to be okay."

"How, Rick? How will everything be okay?"

"I don't know, but it will. I love you too much to lose you."

"But my father..." She has stopped sobbing and is starting to calm down a bit.

"I know. I respect your father. He is a good man. I know he loves you and that you love him. I would never ask you to go against his wishes. We will just not see each other for a while. We can still talk on the phone, and we will think of something."

"I miss you so much already," Lisa says despondently.

"I miss you too. I love you and will never stop loving you. I will do whatever it takes to keep you in my life. We will think of something to change your father's mind. I promise."

After we hang up, I give expression to my true feelings. I feel like my heart is being ripped out of my chest and trampled on. Not my real heart, the defective one that caused all this trouble, but my figurative one, the one that gets glorified on Valentine's Day. It feels even worse than it did when Amy left me. I want to scream and throw things. I want to lie down and cry. I want to punch something. I settle for some really loud music and punch a pillow while crying. Finally, all the fight is out of me, and I just lie on the couch, staring at the ceiling. I don't have any more tears to cry.

I slouch over to the fridge and pull out a bottle of vodka. I pour a large glass and hold it before me, staring into its clear depths. I remember the last time I had tried to drown my sorrows in alcohol. I watch the liquid swirl around hypnotically and try to decide what to do. If I let myself go down this path, to go out and drink away the pain, I might never make it back. It is so hard to climb out of the abyss of depression once you have fallen in. Finally, I set the drink on the counter and pick up my phone. There is one person who has always been there for me. So I dial the number and call Jacob.

"Hello," a voice answers groggily.

I look at the time. It is two in the morning. "I am sorry, I n-n-never should have c-c-called you," I stammer.

"Rick, is that you? Why are you calling so late?"

"Well, I..." My voice cracks, and I pause. I can't bring myself to say it. I am afraid I might start crying again.

"What's the matter?" Jacob asks. I can tell he is wide awake now.

"I didn't know who else to call. Lisa's dad..." My voice cracks again. I swallow back the tears and continue, "Lisa's dad has forbidden her to see me again."

"Oh, man. I'm so sorry to hear that. I'm sure he's just worried about his daughter."

"Yeah, I just don't know what to do, and I just needed to talk to someone. It feels like Amy all over again. But not just Amy. It is like everything all at once. I don't know if I can handle it."

"I'll be right there," Jacob says and hangs up.

I stand at the counter, staring at my phone. I am still staring when there is a knock on my door. Jacob is here. I unbolt the door and let him in. He is in wrinkled sweats, and his hair is sticking up all over. He looks like he got dressed in a hurry. His shirt is backwards. I point at it, and he sheepishly turns it around. I almost smile; I am so glad he has come.

'What's up?' he says, shaking my hand and hugging me all at the same time.

I shrug and lead him over to the couch. I don't even know where to begin. I brush the dirty tissue on to the floor so he has a place to sit. He looks around, taking in the mess, the drink on the counter, and my red eyes.

"That bad, huh?"

"Yeah, that bad. At least she still loves me, whatever that is good for. I can't ask her to defy her dad. It would kill her."

"He is totally adamant about not letting the two of you marry? Did you tell him you are healthy now?"

"He would not listen. I guess it is a case of 'once sick, always sick' with him."

"That's harsh."

We talk for a little while, and in that way, Jacob has turned the conversation to better things without me even noticing. I found that I was talking about business and places I have visited recently. I was even telling him about an upcoming business trip I have planned. I found that I was starting to cheer up.

"Thanks for talking to me. I am feeling so much better," I say.

"That is good. I was worried about you for a while. Look, you have a great future ahead of you. There are so many things you can do. You cannot change everything right now. You may have to be patient, but if Lisa loves you and you love her, things will work out. Don't go wasting your future by letting your past destroy you." I nod, agreeing with Jacob. "You are going to just have to prove to her dad that you are a great guy. It may take some time, but you definitely can't do it if you slip," Jacob says, motioning to the counter and the glass of vodka.

I nod again and vow to myself that I will not let my past destroy my future. I will win over Lisa's dad.

"You know, maybe if you show him how successful you are, then he'll change his mind," Jacob says with a hopeful tint to his voice.

I frown.

"Even if that would work, I don't want to buy my way into their hearts. I want them to truly look at me for who I am and not my disease. Besides, I really believe that my love for her should be enough."

Jacob just shrugs.

I stare out of the window. Even though I believe finding a way to put my will into action is going to be hard, still, I will do whatever it takes. I *will* make him accept me.

I miss Lisa. Phone calls just do not seem to help. I want to see her so bad, but we are still trying to find a way to convince her father that I can take care of her. To make things easier, I have been staying busy. I have been taking on extra projects at work and going to the gym afterwards. I work out until I am exhausted. Then I can fall asleep and get some rest. I feel numb.

I stretch and look around my office. It is a nice office. I have decorated it in the modern style with stainless steel and clean lines. On my desk, I have two monitors to help when I have several windows open at once for a project. One wall is lined with windows, and I can look down over the city skyline. We have expanded the company since I started working here, and we are no longer in the smaller offices near the park. Now we have large offices in the middle of downtown. The walls behind my desk and in front of my desk are solid, and I have put prints of famous modern art on them. One painting is not a print though, and it is this that I love looking at when I am contemplating something. There is something about Dali's art that I love. The last wall has frosted windows and faces the rest of the office. I can see vague outlines of people working hard at their desks. There are smiling pictures of Lisa, my family, friends that I have littered all over the office.

I glance at the clock; it is almost time for me to go to a meeting where I am acting as an advisor to another company. It seems that

I am now considered to be somewhat of an expert in my field. And I've begun to make a name and an income as a consultant. I gather my things and head to the conference room where the meeting will be held. I walk in and take a look around. There are perhaps ten people milling about the room, talking casually. It is a big room, and more people trickle in as I wait. Some are beginning to take spots around the large table that is the centrepiece of the room. There are no decorations and no distractions, except for a lone standard-issue clock on the wall. More people are coming in, and as I watch them walk into the room, my breath catches in my throat. Lisa's father is here!

What should I do? My mind seems to be stuck on this, and I am frozen in place. He glances around and sees me. I can see the recognition in his eyes. For some reason, the fact that he doesn't feel the need to acknowledge me is enough to spur me into action.

"Good morning sir," I say, walking over and shaking his hand. "It is so nice to see you again."

"Likewise," he replies and looks at me as if trying to figure out what I am doing there.

At that moment, the meeting is brought to order, and it is all business. I am introduced as an expert in the field and as someone worth listening to. I then take charge of the meeting and present my message. I have done this so many times now that once I get started, I am comfortable and in my element. Afterwards, I answer questions, and then the meeting is adjourned. Many people come up to me and thank me. I talk to them individually. Finally, there is only one person left – Lisa's dad.

"Great job."

"Thank you sir. I enjoy what I do."

"It seems you are good at it too. You have taught us a lot of new things. I think everyone was impressed with you. I certainly was."

"Thank you. That means a lot to me." It does mean a lot to me. I have been trying to find some way to show him that I am a person worthy of his daughter, and it seems that once again, God has led me to the right place and the right time.

He offers his hand to me, and I make sure to shake it firmly. And as he moves to pull away, I have an idea.

"Sir, if it's not too much of an intrusion, do you mind if I show you something?"

He looks at me suspiciously.

"I promise I won't take much of your time." He sighs and nods in a kind of resignation that lets me know that although I have impressed him with my mind, it doesn't mean that his opinions of me have changed.

I lead him to my office, and when we get there, I watch him take in the luxurious space and the pictures of his daughter smiling and happy.

I steer him to a comfortable chair facing the flat-screen television. Then I move to the TV and place an old and worn DVD that Jacob once gave me in the player.

The programme is a short documentary about aortic valve stenosis. In it, a young attractive man in his late thirties and a man who looks to be in his late sixties are interviewing doctors and patients. They talks about the diagnosis and the treatments and the impact on the lives of people who have AVS. At the end of the video, the younger man discusses his own involvement with AVS and how, although he does not have the condition, someone who is very close to him does. This person he says closed off his life from everyone because he did not want anyone he loved to see him die. Fortunately, one woman was able to convince him to live a full life. He pauses for dramatic effect and then proceeds to reveal that the man in his story is his father and then, to the surprise of the audience, reveals that the older presenter is indeed one and the same person.

The video ends with the father-and-son duo hugging, smiling, and generally full of life.

Throughout the whole video, I am watching Lisa's father as closely as I can without being creepy. In the whole thirty minutes that the video lasts, he has not changed his solemn expression, and now that the video is over, I am almost crazy with a need to see him show any emotion at all. To cover my nervousness, I head to turn off the television. I go as slow as I dare in order to get my nerves under control, and by the time I turn around, I am as composed as ever.

"You're a very persistent man, aren't you?"

The words don't seem annoyed, so I try to smile my most charming smile.

"Well, nothing worth having is easy to get, sir."

He nods once and then heads to the door, and my heart sinks. Even though I know that I have moved a step up in his eyes, I was hoping that he would at least smile at me.

I walk him to his car in complete silence, and my mind is spinning. Before he gets in, he turns to me.

"I am not a cruel man, Rick. I lost my father at a young age, and it devastated our family. I would not wish what my siblings and mother went through on anyone, least of all my daughter. I understand that you care about her. But I am not willing to risk her future for the sake of your happiness. You seem like a good man, but it is my job to ensure that my daughter is taken care of."

"I understand your hesitation sir, but with all due respect, I doubt your mother would have traded the joy I am sure being married to and having children for her husband has brought her for the temporary grief of losing him."

He looks at me for a long while, and I try not to shake in my shoes. His impassive face says nothing of whether or not he is offended. After a long while, he nods sharply, conceding the 'argument'.

He extends his hand one more time, and we shake before he gets in his car and pulls off without a word.

A week later, I am sitting at my desk when my phone rings. The caller ID informs me that it's my doctor. I answer the phone with happiness. Even though we rarely see each other now, I still try to keep in touch with the man who helped me get my life on track.

"Doctor, my doctor!"

"Hello, Rick. How are you?" he responds with a smile in his voice.

"Doing well, thanks. To what do I owe the pleasure of a call?"

"Well, I just had the strangest meeting. A very distinguished man stopped by my office, asking me about you."

"Me?" I say in surprise.

"Yes. He asks me all kinds of questions. About AVS and you in particular. Now normally, I would have told him to speak to one of our junior doctors about AVS and that questions about a patient's medical history are confidential, but I felt in this case it would be best if I answered. I hope I did the right thing."

"It depends on who it was."

"It was Lisa's father."

My heart stops.

"What did you tell him?"

"The truth, that you're completely healthy. I also told him that you are one of the finest young men that I've met. Any man would be lucky to have you as a son."

My heart fills with a mixture of pride and relief.

"Thank you so much, Doc."

"No problem."

We hang up the phone, and my heart fills with joy. Hopefully, I am one step closer to Lisa.

◎

A week later, the phone rings. It is a number I don't recognize.

"Hello."

"May I speak to Rick?" The voice is solemn.

"This is Rick. May I know who's speaking?"

"This is Lisa's father."

"Good afternoon sir. How can I help you, sir?"

"I may have been a little harsh with you, Rick."

"Oh," I say, wondering where this is going.

"I want you to understand that I love my daughter. I only want what is best for her. I did not think you would be that. Now I see that there is more to you than meets the eye."

"I appreciate that, sir."

"In fact, if my daughter would like to continue seeing you, I am okay with that."

My heart stops. I have just been given permission to see Lisa again. I am in such high spirits that I can't help myself. I blurt out, "Sir, I love your daughter and want to marry her. I know it will mean the world to her if you would bless the union."

There is silence, and I worry that I have ruined what I worked so hard to earn. Then he smiles. "Yes, you may have my blessing if you promise to take good care of her and keep her happy."

"I promise," I say, then I pause as an idea has occurred to me. "Would you mind not telling Lisa about my intentions? I want to surprise her."

I can practically hear the smile in his voice as he says, "That will be fine." I smile back. My mind is already calculating how I will ask Lisa.

Later that day, I receive the third in a string of calls that make it the best day of my life. Lisa's familiar number shows up on my phone. She is ecstatic and practically screams over the phone.

"What did you do?"

I laugh. It is so great to hear her happy voice. Over the last few weeks, it has been hell hearing her voice filled with gloomy sadness.

"I told you I'm a miracle worker."

She laughs as well and tells me how her dad came to her and gave her what sounds like the same speech he gave me. We spend the next hour on the phone, just talking about how horrible it has been without being able to see each other.

We make plans for that night, and I decide that this is the night I will ask her to marry me. I do not want to risk anything else coming between us. When we hang up, I am too excited to do anything but go ring-shopping. In the first store, there is nothing I want. It is the same in the second and third stores. Finally, as I am starting to give up hope, I find the perfect ring. I buy it and have it carefully boxed and wrapped. I hold it carefully in my pocket as I walk back to my car. I want to call Lisa right now, but she is working, and I really do want it to be a surprise. I think of all the ways to make it special. Finally, I come up with a plan. It is nothing fancy, just dinner and the question. I think she will like it that way better than a large public announcement.

I am waiting for Lisa to answer the door. Before the door is even completely open, she flings herself at me and wraps me in a huge hug. I hug her back. "I missed you too much," I say. It is the truth. As I hold her, I can smell her hair, and I realize just how much I have missed everything about her.

When we pull up to the building and the valet gets the car, I can see that she realizes where we are going. She has a very surprised look on her face. "We are going here?" she asks incredulously. "I was thinking somewhere a little more casual." She looks down at her pants and T-shirt.

"You look perfect," I assure her and pull her on to the elevator. I press the button labelled floor 29 – The Rainbow Room. The

Rainbow Room is, without argument, the best restaurant in this city. It sits at the top of the skyscraper and rotates, so that while you are eating, you get a panoramic view of the entire city spread out below you. I have never been here before, but I have been told that it is a place where you can have one of the most romantic dinners. When the elevator doors open, we both just stand in the doorway, awestruck. The restaurant is bathed in the light of the setting sun. The room is decorated in yellow and gold. Right now, the gold embellishments are tinged pink and purple, reflecting the sunset outside. It is breathtaking. There are trees and multicoloured floral arrangements isolating each table but still allow a perfect view through the windows. We follow the hostess in silence to our table.

At first, the perfectness around us keeps us silent. Then Lisa says something and I reply and we can't stop talking. The waiter brings us our meal, and it sits untouched until it is only slightly warm before we pause long enough to try it. When we finish, I grow silent. Now is the moment.

"Lisa," I say. "I want to ask you something."

"Yes," she says.

I pull out the box and set it on the table. "Lisa, will you marry me?"

"Rick!" She picks up the box and slowly opens it to stare at the ring. "Yes, Rick, I will marry you!" She is almost lit up with excitement. Then her face falls. She closes the box and sets it in the middle of the table. "I can't, Rick. My father. It would kill him if I married without his permission."

"I know," I say. I pause for dramatic effect. "He gave me permission yesterday."

"What? How?"

I tell her everything about the meeting and talking to her dad. As I talk, I hold her hand in mine. "So I would love to marry you if you will have me," I say, sliding the ring onto her finger.

She is crying now. Tears of joy are sliding down her face. "Yes, Rick, I love you."

It turns out proposing is the easiest part of getting married. Lisa and I have set a date for this winter. We have spent every free minute sending out invitations, counting responses, getting photos taken, picking out colours and cakes, and an infinite number of things that is seems are essential to a wedding. It is not all business though. Sometimes we sneak away from all the craziness and take slow walks through the park. These are my favourite moments. We daydream together about what our life will be like. We build towering castles in the clouds. Our children will be perfect and well behaved. Our home will be large and in a nice neighbourhood. Even our dog will be the most obedient dog on the block. We are going to have the perfect life.

I wake up to the sounds of people milling around the house. It is my wedding day, and all my relatives are here to share in my special moment. I lie in bed and just listen to the bustle. I am comfortable. Despite my excitement about today, I feel a little bit of fear that things will not go perfectly.

"Time to get up," my uncle calls, banging on my door. "You don't want to be late to your own wedding." I glance at my clock. I still have a few hours before I need to go. I also have a lot to do. I stretch my arms and head to the shower.

We have decided to wear the traditional Indian clothes for our wedding. I dress in a gold Jodhpuri. Lisa helped me pick it out. The hems are covered in intricate embroidery representing health, happiness, and a long life. I think that it makes me look dignified but too serious, so I add a red scarf to look happy. Once I am dressed and have all my accessories on, we all walk together in one big party to the Johnson's home.

I look out over the crowd gathered around me. I see so many friends and family members. Jacob smiles at me and winks. I am reminded of all the things that we have been through together. My life has not always been perfect, but I am so glad I have been given it. I see now that my trials have brought me to this point. They have shaped me into the man I am, a man who is surrounded by good friends and family, and who will soon be married to a wonderful woman. The music changes, and I look up to see Lisa enter. She is breathtaking. Her black hair is pulled back and covered by a red veil. Her sari is gold like my jacket, but covered in red beads and embroidery. She has a large jewel in the centre of her forehead, just above where her bindi will go. Jewels dot her eyes, and large earrings dangle from her ears. Every inch of skin on her arms and palms is covered in intricate henna. She is looking down as all good Indian brides do, but then she glances up, catches my eye, and smiles before looking down again. I have to remind myself to breathe. I cannot believe I am going to marry the woman of my dreams. I am still smiling as her father, uncles, and every male relative she has, lead her to me and place her hand in mine.

The ceremony is a blur of vows and rituals. I am so excited, I am having trouble with the simplest concepts. Then we are at the part where I actually have to say something. I listen closely as Lisa promises to honour, love, and care for me in sickness and in health, for richer or for poorer. These words have special significance for us. We never know when she might have to live up to that promise. Then it is my turn.

"Rick," the priest says, "do you promise to take Lisa to have and to hold, from this day forward, for better or for worse, for richer, for poorer, in sickness and in health, to love and to cherish from this day forward until death?"

I look at Lisa. With all the love I feel, I declare, "I do."

Epilogue

Ten years have passed since Lisa and I got married. We have had ups and downs, like any married couple, but we have always stayed together. After about three years of marriage, I started experiencing heart pains again. We went into the hospital filled with fear. However, after doing lots of tests, the doctors assured me that the problem could be solved by taking a different class of medication. I have been on the new medicine since, and I am doing fine. The doctors still monitor my condition, but less frequently, and there is less worry. Business has been good, and we have bought a house in the suburbs about halfway between our parents. The house is perfect for us. It has two storeys, three bedrooms, and a big backyard with two maple trees. It is in a quiet subdivision near a park that the kids love to play on. Sometimes at night, in the summer, we sit out on the front porch and count the stars.

I still can't believe that I have kids, and not just one, but two of them. We were scared to have kids at first. We worried that I would pass on the gene that led to my aortic valve stenosis. We spent a lot of time online, doing research and talking to our doctor. Finally, we were assured that not only were the chances of our child having the condition pretty low, but that medicine had advanced and now there was no reason for the child to not have a normal childhood. This was very important to me. I did not want to always be stopping my child in his moment of exuberance or worrying that a race on the playground could kill him. So with some trepidation and a whole lot of hope, we had Jane. She was so much fun and such a blessing that we decided to have one more. A few years later, Mike was born. They are both completely healthy.

I am climbing the stairs to my children's bedroom; it is my turn to check on them. I gently open the door. The room is dark and silent. I can make out two still forms on the bunk bed. Jane and Mike are sleeping soundly. Their breath comes slow and steady. Their hair spreads around their heads like a dark halo on the pillow. Mike is three. He is sleeping, wrapped around his teddy bear. Jane, who is six, sprawls out on her bed, her hand stretched over her head. I can smell the gentle fragrance of their lavender soap from their bath. They had a long day today, playing at the park. Jane loves the swings and is always calling to go higher. Mike loves the slides. I have never seen such a daredevil. He even tries sliding down slides while standing up. When I watch them, I experience waves of nostalgia for the childhood I never had. I also experience great satisfaction in watching them run and play and knowing they are safe. In their bedroom, I look at them and wonder if they are happy. I debate going over and covering them up. No, it is warm enough in the room, and I don't want to wake them. I gently shut the door and offer a prayer of gratitude that my children are both healthy.

I go back to the living room. Lisa is reading. I stop for a minute to admire her beauty and the peace she radiates. She has started to get a few white hair of her own; they add character to her braid. If I look closely, I can see that her face has a few lines, but they are smile lines and I am glad to see them there. It means that her life has been one of happiness. Despite the fine lines and white hair (or maybe because of them), she is still as beautiful to me as the day we were married. I bend down and kiss her. "I love you," I say.

"I love you too. Are they finally asleep?"

"Yes, they were pretty worn-out. They had a lot of excitement today."

"They needed to get out. It has been rainy all week, and I think they were going to burst with energy."

"It was a great day. Thank you for planning it, rabbit."

"Are you going to write your letter?"

"I am just trying to think of how to say the things I want today." I look at her. "Did you already finish?"

"I wrote mine while you were giving the kids a bath."

Every year on our children's birthdays, we write them a letter to let them know how much we love them. We plan to give the letters to them when they turn sixteen.

I sit at my desk, lean back in my chair, and contemplate my life. The last ten years have been so good to me. I have learned so many things since I was young. I made a lot of mistakes, but I have made some good choices, and the Lord has blessed me. I can see his guiding hand everywhere as I look back. I don't know what will happen to me as I get older, so I have taken the time to write letters to my children on their birthdays so they will always know I love them. Today, we celebrate Jane's sixth birthday. I am trying to write down the wisdom I have learned through experience. I open the programme and start typing.

Dear Jane,

I love you so much. You and your brother are more important to me than anything else in this world. As I watched you blow out your candles today, I thought about how much you have grown since your mom and I brought you home from the hospital. You were so tiny and helpless. I worried I would drop you or break you if I held you too tight. We had to do everything for you. Now you are so big. You do many things for yourself. There is so much of life you have left to experience, so many things you need to learn. I hope I can teach you most of them. If there was anything I would have you learn, it would be these five things.

First, it is important to get a good education. But having a degree in your hand does not make you a better person. It does not even make you a well-qualified person. What really matters in life are your abilities and your determination to reach a goal. John Calvin Coolidge, a former president of the United States, said it better. He said, "Nothing in the world can take the place of persistence. Talent will not; nothing is more common than unsuccessful men with talent. Genius will not; unrewarded genius is almost a proverb. Education alone will not; the world is full of educated derelicts. Persistence and determination alone are omnipotent. The slogan 'press on' has solved and always will solve the problems of the human race."

You have to set a goal and then work really hard to obtain it. You have to press on. Don't set low goals either. Set goals that will stretch you, that will lift you up and make you better. Having determination is what counts in this life.

Second, never judge someone by their health. So many times in life, people won't associate with others who are not like them. Do not make this mistake. I was sick a lot when I was little, and no one would ever play with me since I could not run around like them. I spent a lot of time just watching life. If you see someone like that, go and be their friend. Our health does not matter. Even if you are healthy now, you could lose it tomorrow. It is the pure hearts that we have that matter. Cultivate yours, and look for it in others. Your mom is so good at this. When I first told her I was sick, she just smiled and told me she loved me because of who I am. Watch her, and try to be like her.

Third, never let a problem get you down. It is so easy to go through life thinking, Woe is me. I have such a hard life. But this kind of thinking does not solve anything. It only makes matters worse. It leads to a never-ending spiral of depression and rejection. The only way to find happiness is to face your problems with a smile on your face. Dan Millman once said, "Act happy, feel happy, be happy, without a reason in the world." Do not wait until you have a reason to be happy. Instead, smile through your problems, and you will find that your problems are smaller. People will also like to be around you. For a while I went around thinking only about my difficulties. I hated myself and life. Then a good friend helped me see past all that. He helped me realize that laughter really is the best medicine. It is true; when I faced my problems with an attitude of happiness, I started recovering better, and I found happiness. People started to like being near me, and I met your mom.

Fourth, never blame your problems on god. More often than not, it is our fault we have a problem in the first place. Sometimes, though, god does give us a problem. It does not matter if he gives us a small problem or a large problem; we should always see it as a blessing. He is testing us, trying to see if we can handle it. When we do, he has a blessing for us. Look at your problems as a way to prove you are ready for a blessing. Gandhi said, "My imperfections and failures are as much a blessing from god as my successes and my talents and I lay them both at his feet." To god we do not need to be perfect at everything; we just need to continue trying to be.

Finally, if you allow yourself to become seduced by fear and insecurity, you only sabotage your own happiness. Fear and insecurity are like two little devils who sit on your shoulder and whisper in your ear things they want you to believe. They want nothing more than for you to believe that you can't do that or you aren't good enough. If you listen to these devils, you won't try, and then you will fail. The next time you will be more scared and you'll fail again. It is a self-fulfilling prophecy. When you hear those little devils start to whisper their lies, do not listen. Instead, tell yourself that you are good enough and that you can do it. Then try and you will find that you can do it. You will find happiness in doing this.

I know that is a lot of information, so here are the bullet points.

First, education is important, but an academic degree is not the solution to everything. What counts are your ability and your determination. You must have a desire to reach your goal. Second, health should not be the only factor to a relationship with friends or a loved one. Always look on the inside of people and see who they really are. Third, do not let your problems get you down. Always make the choice to be happy and face your life with a smile. Fourth, no matter what problems we face, big or small, do not blame God for it. God uses trials to test our will, and when we prove ourselves, he has something much better in store for us than we could ever dream of. Finally, allowing the devils of fear and insecurity to seduce you leads you down a spiral of negativity. It becomes a self-fulfilling prophecy of sabotage.

If you remember these things, you will be spared a lot of the heartache I experienced. It is my hope that your life is always a blessed and happy one.
Always remember that I love you.

Love,

Your dad

I print the letter. At the bottom, I sign my name and draw a small picture for her. Right now, her favourite animal is a horse, so I do my best to draw a stick horse with a little girl feeding it a carrot. It is rough, but I write a small description underneath. I finish and carefully fold the letter. I place it with Lisa's letter and tuck both into the envelope with the letters from past years. Then I stand up and place the quickly thickening envelope on the bookshelf near the photo albums. I stretch out my back; I am getting stiff in my old years.

I walk over to Lisa and kiss her on the forehead. "Are you coming to bed, dear?" I ask.

"In a minute, I just want to finish this." I smile and wonder if by *this* she means the chapter or the book.

"I will get your toothbrush ready for you."

"Thanks," she says, looking up briefly.

As I get ready for bed, my heart is full with the blessings I have. I could not ask for anything more. I have lived a blessed life, problems and all.

That night, as I close my eyes, I realize god has given me a great gift, one that I am just now starting to see. It is this: In foolishness, I have gained wisdom. By falling, I have risen. In rebelling against god, I have accepted him. By stammering, I have learned to speak. And by hating, I have learned to love.

Recommended Reading

Her Last Wish
Ajay K Pandey

His father's over expectations only ruined his self-confidence further with each failure. A ray of hope walked into his life as his wife. Everything is going per plan, when he finds out that she does not have much time to live and takes it upon himself to fight all odds – even his family, if need be – to help her fight her medical condition.

Her Last Wish is an inspiring story of love, relationships and sacrifice.

Ajay is the bestselling author of *You are the Best Wife* and has won many hearts with his writing. He is also actively involved in working for social causes.

ISBN: 978-9382665878; Price: 175/-; Pages: 208; Binding: Paperback.

You are my Reason to Smile
Arpit Vageria

Ranbir is a dreamer. He has a well-paying job, is a good lover, an ideal son, but he is not happy. Because his true calling is not in the corporate; it's in writing. Amidst all this confusion, Pihu Sharma enters his life – his first ever fan, who seems to be head over heels in love with him. Join Ranbir as he makes his way through a world that kills for money and dies for love.

Arpit Vageria is a bestselling author of *I Still Think About You*. He also writes for the Indian television industry, and enjoys road trips, singing, playing pranks and adventurous sports.

ISBN: 978-9382665885; Price: 175/-; Pages: 184; Binding: Paperback.

Promise Me A Million Times
Keshav Aneel

Like a couple of migratory birds, both Charlie and Edwin leave to settle in the big city. For Edwin, it was to chase his dreams of becoming an actor; but for Charlie, it was just to be with his only friend.

Life throws Charlie in Aster's way. He could never have guessed, but he was in for an absolute unthoughtful phase of profoundness, which was going to last forever.

Keshav Aneel is a young marketing professional, who chose to do his heart's bidding and ended his brief corporate career to immerse himself into his creative side.

ISBN: 978-93-82665-73-1; Price: 175/-; Pages: 168; Binding: Paperback.

No Matter What I Do
Devanshi Sharma

Kabir, Amaira, Kushank and Suhani – four very different people bound together by love and friendship – are struggling to find the motto of their lives. Four threads entangled together and four lives recuperating each other – *No Matter What I Do* is the story of these four youngsters, on a journey to find themselves and how they reverse stereotypes on the way.

Devanshi Sharma is a twenty-one-year-old dreamer from Indore and strongly believes in hope. She enjoys talking, writing, dancing and eating, and her family is her lifeline.

ISBN: 978-9382665847; Price: 175/-; Pages: 200; Binding: Paperback.